D
A
V
I
D

Do Plátanos Go Wit' Collard Greens?

L
A
M
B

I WRITE WHAT I LIKE, INC.
P.O. Box 30
New York, N.Y. 10268-0030
1994

Grateful acknowledgement is made for permission to reprint from:

Dominicans Have Had Their Riots of Passage, by Frank Batista. Copyright © 1992 by Frank Batista. Reprinted with permission of Frank Batista.

From Columbus to Castro: The History of the Caribbean, by Eric Williams. Copyright © 1970 by Eric Williams. Reprinted by permission of the publisher.

"Gription," from _Big Bank Take Little Bank_ by Paul Beatty. Copyright © 1991 by Paul Beatty. Reprinted by permission of Paul Beatty.

In Goode Faith, by W. Wilson Goode with Joann Stevens. Copyright © 1992 Judson Press. Reprinted with the permission of the publisher.

Native Stranger, by Eddy L. Harris. Copyright © 1992 by Eddy L. Harris. Reprinted by permission of Simon & Schuster, Inc.

'Rudy's narrow win clouds sign of rainbow,' by Jim Sleeper. Copyright © 1993 The New York Daily News, L.P.. Reprinted with permission of the publisher.

To the Most High for listening to my prayers.

To my mother and grandmother for raising me, and for encouraging me to read from day one.

To all of my uncles for acting as my composite father, and for teaching me to love myself and my people.

Vece, for not letting me be lazy.

Oh yeah, Ralph how many times have you read <u>Bury My Heart At Wounded Knee</u>?

Special thanx to all of my advance readers:

Alexei, Alim, Dawn, Grace, Jaye,
                    Marcus, Nsinga, Ray, Terrence,
(if I forgot anyone, please forgive me)

"Why are people of color always the victims of police brutality?. . .Why doesn't the gun go off in John Gotti's back or the mafia's back or someone in the suburbs? We don't shoot people; they, the police, are the animals."

Al Sharpton, 1992
Washington Heights Protest

"We must face the fact that our race is not European; it is rather a composite of Africa and America rather than an emanation of Europe for Spain, itself, ceased to be European by its African blood; its institutions and character."

Simon Bolivar
First Venezuelan President

"I am 67 . . . a Hispanic of dark skin, known among Hispanics as mulatto, and among Anglo-Saxons as black. . . . Passing by a gathering of Giuliani supporters in Queens, I stayed . . . Once in a while a black person walked by us and yelled to me: "Hey, you! you! . . . You are black! What are you doing there?" This went on until I shouted back: "Yes, I know I am black, but also Hispanic! This is why!""

Letter to the editor
New York Newsday
October 11, 1993

"If you lived in this neighborhood,
      you would hate the cops too."
Michael Dowd, corrupt cop
Mollen Commission Hearings, 1993

He had a sinking feeling. Cops all over the city were p.o.'d. Corrupt cops were reacting to the pain of the truth stepping on their toes, while honest cops felt as if all cops were being painted with the broad brush of corruption. Meanwhile, those damn Black and Latino activists had asked for Dinkins' and Giuliani's support for the appointment of a special prosecutor to investigate the beating. Under the confluence of these converging events desperation set in as they felt the walls closing in, and frantically searched for a way out.

"Kill the mayor! Huh, I don't know about that one . . . "

"Look, you guys, I've got a cousin on the force down in Philadelphia and he told me a few years back how they were going to take care of that nigger mayor down there. . . . We could do the same thing here, create a riot situation, it's election time, Dinkins has to come. And boom! Out of nowhere a shot is fired from somebody in the crowd, down goes Stinkins."

"But, . . ."

"But, nothing. We've got all this heat coming down on us. First you idiots beat up that curly haired nigger, and now they're pressing Dinkins to investigate. The damn Mollen Commission he appointed is snooping around everywhere. Look I'm telling you we get rid of Dinkins and all of this goes away. With Rudy in office, do you think he's going to give a fuck? Nah, Rudy loves the police."

Chapter Two

When Freeman Woodson became editor and chief of 'The Shield', Hunter College's Black student newspaper, he saw himself as walking in the footsteps of his intellectual hero, Steve Biko, the South African student leader and political activist. Like Biko, Freeman was, so to speak, nice with the pen. And like his hero, he demanded quality writing, quality research and quality scholarship from his staff. The kind of quality they could only attain by bringing the same commitment to writing well for the paper, that they had to summon up to pass Expository Writing, the freshmen English class that so terrified Hunter's black student populace.

For the first issue to be published under his editorial leadership, Freeman was committed to be being bold, provocative and illuminating. And now that the Fall semester had begun, he was determined to convince the Shield's editorial board to devote the entire first issue of the semester to the question of police brutality and the role and performance of the Civilian Complaint Review Board, an issue most of them believed settled when Mayor Dinkins, New York City's first Black mayor, convinced the City Council to pass a bill creating the board the year before. Freeman, however, had recently read that Rudolph Giuliani (or Rudy, though not the "Rudy" of movie fame, President Clinton, sir), Dinkins' nemesis from the '89 election, and his opponent in the present mayoral race was looking to resurrect the debate. A year earlier, Giuliani had been blasted in the local press for egging the police on in their protest-turned-riot in and around the area of City Hall. A riot in which some officers, sworn to uphold the law, actually tried to storm City Hall. Other officers blocked the Brooklyn Bridge. And still others held up racially offensive signs attacking the Mayor, harassed passers-by and where one uniformed officer reportedly called councilwoman Una Clarke a "nigger," and refused to allow her to enter City Hall.

Now as they discussed the contents and format of the issue, the research skills Freeman had first become acquainted with in the course of watching his father doing background research for journal articles and in preparation for lectures as a political science professor at City College, were bearing fruit. As a young black man growing up in New York, Freeman had had enough confrontations with biased police officers to already be concerned about police brutality. His interest and passion regarding the issue had been heightened, however, by the April, '92 meltdown in Los Angeles. And his heightened passion had been further fueled by the June, '92 explosion in New York. An explosion which saw riots erupt over a forty square block area in Washington Heights, resulting in at least one death, fifteen injuries, and extensive property damage in the form of overturned cars, destroyed storefronts, looted stores and random destruction. He had paid particular attention to the Washington Heights disturbance as it happened in New York, and as it had forced him to confront the rapid growth of the City's Latino population generally, and its Dominican population particularly.

The first night of rioting in Washington Heights, Freeman was engrossed with the news reports, as he videotaped frantic white voices reporting with horror that Los Angeles had come to New York. Because a year had passed since Washington Heights exploded, Freeman decided to play a copy of the video so as to refresh memories, and to stir emotions in order to ensure everyone's wholehearted commitment to the job ahead.

"Like ta hear it? Here it go."
He was an 'In Living Color' fan.

> "Bands of people chanting "Killer Cop"
> and "Justice" in Spanish have been
> marching through the streets. Earlier in
> the evening it was reported over police
> radio that a police helicopter was struck
> by gun fire and had to return to its base
> One man fell five stories to his death
> after being pursued across a rooftop at
> 172nd Street and Audubon Avenue by
> officers who said they'd seen him
> throwing bottles. There have been reports
> that earlier this evening a man was
> pulled from his car and beaten at West
> 168th Street and Audubon Avenue. Amid the
> wreckage, residents turned a section of
> 162nd Street into a memorial to Jose
> Garcia, the man shot by police tonight.
> A spontaneous vigil saw a crowd use
> hundreds of white candles to write
> his nickname, "Kiko"."

The video continued as angry rioters vented their rage:

> "The people aren't gonna take
>   it anymore, they wanna be
>   treated like human
>   beings, that's
>   all they want."

> "The cops think it's a joke . . . and
> they wanna go home like it's just a job

> for them, but tonight it's not
>   just a job for them,
>   the type of anger they created
>   in this community,
>   they gonna have to reap,
>   they gonna reap what they sow."

Meanwhile, with New York City about to hold the Democratic National Convention, Mayor Dinkins issued this appeal for calm:

> "Whatever, happens, the appropriate
> response is not violence which could only
> result in further injury and maybe loss
> of life . . ."

"You, see what I'm saying?" Freeman asked without waiting for an answer. "This was not a minor disturbance, the reporter said that the rioting had occurred over a forty square block radius! I mean, come on, a police helicopter was shot and had to return to its base! This is an issue we as students, shit, as black people, we need to be involved in. How many times are you trying to get home from a late class only to have to deal wit' some Long Island whiteboy tryin' to be John Wayne and fuckin' wit' you for no reason? I know you know what I'm talkin' about, because we've discussed it when it's happened in the past, and it's happened far too often for us to not do something about it. Now Mayor Dinkins, whatever you or I might think of him, pushed through this Civilian Complaint Review Board, and you and I need to give the Board our support in order to make sure that it continues to exist as it exists or in a better form, by using the paper to advocate and promote that support and by takin' the lead in organizin' students to protest against any Giuliani proposal to do away wit' the Board."

"Well, before we talk about protesting can we finish talking about what this issue is going to look like?" Asked Sherry A. Moore. Sherry was Freeman's ex-girlfriend, at least that's what everyone thought, but for Sherry and Freeman, it was unclear; it was clear that there was still some tension between them, but whether it was romantic tension or give me some space tension, they hadn't quite worked out yet.

"Thank you Sherry, you always did have a way of bringin' me back down to earth. Well, as far as this issue is concerned, I think we need to take a multi-pronged approach. First off, I think we need to do a history of police brutality cases in the City. As far as I'm concerned, it's so bad that even if we just stick to the last decade, shit, the last five years alone, we'll be able to emphatically and dramatically make our case. Second, we need to explore and explain what the Board is and what it's designed to accomplish, give the proposal its props where props are due and criticize it where it needs to be criticized."

"Aren't you forgetting politics?"

"Well actually, Sherry, that's the part I thought you'd be good at writin' seein' as how much you like conflict and all. You could tell us the players, tell us who's for the Board as it is, and who's against it, for instance, why Mr. Giuliani . . ."

"Oh please!"

"takes the stand he does on this issue."

"Er, excuse me Freeman, it's two o'clock some of us do have to get to class, I mean we don't want to be late on the first day, now do we?"

"Oops! I'm sorry, thanks My-Lady, I mean Me-Lady, I mean Malady (Malady's mother had just finished watching Robin Hood moments before going into labor, and with memories of the heroic men in tights prancing in her head, she wanted to name her daughter after the most prominent damsel in distress, Maid Marianne. Unfortunately she couldn't remember her name, only that people referred to her as milady. Mistaking her title for her name, she set forth to name her daughter 'Milady', unfortunately, her poor spelling rendered it 'Malady') sometimes I get a little long winded, you know how we American born Africans can be. We'll meet back here at 4:30? Okay? Later, peace."

Chapter Three

"So, Sherry why don't you walk me to class and help me give the teacher an apple?"

"No, I don't think so, I have my own class to go to thank you."

"And which class would that be?"

"Accounting."

"Oh good then, that means it's in Hunter College West, I'm headin' in that direction too."

"I thought you were going to meet O.K.?"

"I am, we're gonna meet over by the escalator, after my Spanish class, so come on. Oh, and by the way, I must say that your braids are lookin' quite lovely today, my dear, 'quite smashing I would say in fact'. (He added in his best English accent.) How long you goin' to keep them in?"

"Well since I'm working on campus this semester, I'll probably keep them in the whole semester. Next semester now is another story child, I've got an internship

at J.P. Morgan and I am not going in there looking like
Angela Davis."

"Don't you think that's kind of hypocritical?"

"Listen Freeman, are you going to be walking into
one of those big law firms wearing a red, black, and green
tie? No. So, please don't trip, sisters have got it hard
enough."

As Freeman and Sherry weaved their way through
the crowd, the halls were filled with beginning of the year
anticipation. Freshmen heading in the wrong direction;
Seniors scrambling to get into that special course that
would allow them to meet the school's notorious
distribution requirements, so that they could graduate in the
Spring; and eighth-year sophomores lounging, cooling,
chilling on the third floor walkway, where Freeman was to
meet O.K., chewing the fat, shooting the shit, taking up
space, without really mattering, and passively watching the
world go by. Who knew? In another eight years, they
might actually graduate.

Freeman and O.K. had been boys since they'd
persevered through English 120 together in their freshmen
year. O.K. was a dee jay/m.c., he couldn't make up his
mind as to which one. He preferred being a dee jay, but he
saw more money in rocking the mic - you could say he was
a wannabee D.J. Quik, but with some Afrocentric
consciousness. He was planning to go to the Stern Business
School at N.Y.U., while Freeman was planning on going
to N.Y.U.'s Law School. The long range plan was to open
their own record company, O.K. Records. At the moment,
O.K. was busy brainstorming for his first album, 'A -
O.K.', and his first single, 'I'm O.K., You're Okay'. More
often than their plans, however, Freeman and O.K.'s
conversations frequently revolved around one topic -
women. And the beginning of the semester was an

especially ripe time for holding such discussions, as they'd rush back excitedly from class, anxious to both give and receive a report on the new crop of freshmen, transfer students, and sistas they'd just somehow previously missed. This day, once he got around to it, Freeman was going to have a particularly interesting report for O.K..

Chapter Four

"Yo', Freeman, what up?! What up?!"
O.K. asked, as he raised his right hand, palm open, thumb pointed heavenly, with his pinkie finger pointing toward the earth and his index and middle fingers rushing to meet Freeman's hand as they formed an open peace sign ready to go into "all that post grip flip wilson royal order of the water buffalo [type] shit," that Paul Beatty so brilliantly captured in his poetic hit 'Gription'. Like Beatty's protagonist, however, Freeman wasn't sure which shake O.K. was looking to make, so as O.K.'s hand soared through the air Freeman "improvised [his] handshake guise and just bang[ed] fists." O.K. was pissed. He was a man living in the wrong era, he would have been great on a Vietnam dap line.

"Wussup, O.K., what are you so excited about?"
"Yo', wussup, Freeman, you call that a handshake?"
"Yo', c'mon dude, chill."
"Ah-ight, ah-ight, yo', who was that honey I saw you kickin' it to at the pizza parlor this afternoon?"
"What honey?" Freeman responded with a sly smile.
"Don't eee-even front, you know who I'm talkin' 'bout, brown skin, sorta Puerto Rican/Indian lookin' chick."

"O-Oh her," Freeman said, feigning surprise.

"Yes, her, who was that?" O.K. asked with a sense of urgency.

"This Dominican babe from my Spanish class."

"This Dominican babe, does she have a name?"

"Angelita."

"So wuss - up?!" Inquired O.K., with his arms and hands flailing a la Arsenio.

"Yo', I don't know, man, she came up a little short."

"A little short?! A little short?! Lookin' like dat! What do you mean she came up a little short?"

"Well, I'm not gonna lie, when I first saw her I, like you, was all in, but that was until she told me about her parents."

"Her parents? What the fuck did she say?" An incredulous O.K. asked, unable to fathom what Angelita could possibly have said to justify Freeman's statement.

Recognizing O.K.'s shock at his lack of enthusiasm, Freeman explained how he had asked Angelita what her parents looked like. How she had said that her mother basically looked like her, only a little lighter, and how she had said that her father was a little darker than her with sort of bad hair, not that bad, she had rushed to say, just sort of bad.

"Sorta bad hair?!" O.K. asked, with his face twisted in confusion and revulsion.

"Word, I was buggin'," Freeman said with his face likewise twisted, "*youknowwhatah'msayin'*, cauz up till then I was hopin' she was deep, but when she started talkin' about good and bad hair, I figured she had nothing in her head but air, but dare I say her beauty was rare, so I didn't care to be antagonistic, so I flipped it, switched it, kept kickin' ballistics, smoothly, fluently, gassin' her up,

G, cauz she was crazy phat, see, so I had to come correct like the mickity, mickity mack, in fact, Black, it was sorta like a Bruce Lee flick -- cauz that's how hard I was kickin' it to honey dip!"

"Yo', that's how hard you had better keep kickin' it." O.K. reasserted having been buoyed by Freeman's linguistic dexterity. "I mean that good hair shit was bugged! But shit, she can learn, but you cain't teach beauty like dat, homeboy!"

"Yeah, you might be right. She definitely seemed interested, maybe I'll see what's up."

"Now you talkin'."

Chapter Five

ON THE FIRST DAY OF THE REST OF HER LIFE, ANGELITA DE CIMARRONES, had gotten up at six-thirty in the morning bright, cheery eyed, and anxious to get to her first class. She'd dreamed of being a doctor since she was a little girl, and this morning she was thrilled that her dream was that much closer to becoming a reality.

Angelita's parents had come to Nueva York from the Dominican Republic in 1967, eight years later Angelita's birth greeted the Big Apple. And now her parents looked forward to the day when their little Angel would fulfill their dreams by becoming the first person in her family to attend college.

As Angelita finished dressing, she looked in the mirror with a smile of satisfaction and also apprehension. She was proud that she was going to college. Proud even though some of her friends, and even her sister, thought she was crazy for not just going to work, but she was also nervous about the experience, and as was her wont when she was nervous she twirled her long shiny straight, but wavy, deep ink black hair. She tried in vain to brush away her fears with the comb, to soothe her butterflies by massaging vaseline into her magnificently full and moist lips. Sometimes, when she was particularly anxious, she would calm herself by saturating her naturally beautiful honey complexion in baby oil, but there wasn't anytime to do that this day, she had to get to school. Now, as she looked at her reflection, it looked back inquisitively, as if it had just realized that she reflected in her appearance, the history of the Dominican Republic, her parents' homeland and the source of New York City's latest mass immigration.

The Dominican Republic was originally inhabited by the indigenous population of this hemisphere whom Columbus labeled Indians in his mistaken belief that he had reached Asia-- you know the tune,

'in 1492 Columbus sailed the ocean blue',
and he and his crew
stumbled   upon   the   island   he   labeled
Hispaniola,
then a few years later the Spanish ran it
over.'

The Spanish who'd financed Columbus' voyage were driven by a mad desire for gold, and Columbus was eager to satiate their lust. While in the Bahamas, he noticed that some of the people wore gold rings in their noses. And according to Eric Williams' excellent history of the Caribbean 'From Columbus to Castro', Columbus wrote in his journal that:

"Without doubt . . . there is in these
lands a vast quantity of gold, and the
Indians I have on board do not speak
without reason when they say that in
these islands, there are places where
they dig out gold, and wear it on their
necks, ears, arms and legs . . ."

In a 1493 letter Columbus assured an investor that
the Indians' land was dotted with vast gold mines.
Eventually the island became the center of the Caribbean
sugar economy, which soon spread to Puerto Rico, Cuba
and Jamaica. Within three years of Columbus' arrival, the
Spaniards had launched war on the Indians. Armed only
with arrows and bows the Indians were overmatched foes
for the crossbows, knives, artillery, calvary and savage
dogs of the Spanish. Defeated and destitute, the Indians
existing near the mines were forced to pay the Spanish,
"from one-half to two-thirds of an ounce of gold every
three months." Those Indians surviving elsewhere had to
pay twenty-five pounds of cotton. Subjugated, and defeated
the Indians fled to the mountains. Now siphoned off in land
unsuited for the necessary cultivation, the Indians began to
starve to death. In a desperate attempt to appease the
Spanish' seemingly insatiable greed, one of the Indian
leaders offered to put an elephantine plot of land under
grain cultivation if Columbus would just stop demanding
gold. Columbus refused, but cut the payment by half. A
couple of years later to satisfy his men's greed, Columbus
ganked the Indians' land and gave it to his men complete
with Indian slave labor. Steadily, inevitably the population
was being decimated and eradicated. Horribly, incredibly
by 1570 only two villages survived in Hispaniola of the

people of whom Columbus had written "there is no better nor gentler people in the world."

With ten little Indians dwindled down to two, Indian labor had to be replaced. In 1517, the first asiento was entered into for the enslavement of African people. By 1540 more than thirty thousand kidnapped Africans, among them Nya, Angelita's great ancestress and the primogenitor of the de Cimarrones' African roots, were carted into Hispaniola. The thievery was so great that the Spanish historian Herrera in his 'History of the Indies' wrote "there are so many Negroes in this island, as a result of sugar factories, that the land seems an effigy or an image of Ethiopia itself." In 1942 J.A. Rogers wrote that "[i]f Haiti [the Dominican Republic's neighbor] is the Negro Republic then [the Dominican Republic] is the mulatto one."

Today in New York, hundreds of thousands of sons and daughters of Africa by way of the Dominican Republic are settling into Washington Heights and other areas of the city. One, very special one, was going to settle into Freeman's arms, soon, if he had anything to say about it.

Chapter Six

Aside from his love life, however, Freeman still had a paper to put out, classes to attend and a law school entrance exam to study for. He figured that he'd probably catch some flack from the school's administration for the Shield's coverage, so he wanted to make sure every article was thoroughly researched. Later that week he was greatly pleased by the reports he got at a follow up meeting.

"Freeman, look at this article I found in Newsday about the Washington Heights riots. I'll read part of it to

you, it's by Frank Batista, a Dominican who grew up in
East New York:

> "For years, Dominicans and other Latinos
> have protested police brutality
> peacefully . . . four years ago, after
> the beating death of Dominican Juan
> Rodriguez [a]bout 2,000 Latinos gathered
> in Williamsburg in non-violent protest.
> Although [there were] indictments of
> three of the four police officers
> involved, all were . . . acquitted. . . .
> [During the Washington Heights protest] I
> overheard a group of young Dominicans say
> . . . "Remember . . . Manuel Marte?
> Nothing was ever done about that." Marte
> was a neighborhood boy beaten unconscious
> by police in 1988 in a case of mistaken
> identity. He lost two teeth and needed
> five stitches. Riots might have occurred
> [last spring], when a Dominican
> restaurateur in Brooklyn was shot six
> times and killed by officers responding
> to a disturbance. Riots could have
> occurred . . . in December, 1990, when
> witnesses saw a TNT officer shoot and
> kill a defenseless youth, Daniel Felix
> Zapata, outside a bodega. Riots might
> have occurred last October, when two
> officers from the 34th . . . killed an
> Ecuadorean, Thomas Vizueta. The Latino
> Rights Project has documented more than
> 40 cases of police brutality against
> Latinos since 1988. "So when Dominicans

chanted "Policia, asesinos," and "No
justicia, no paz," they meant it. . . ."

"I hear that, Malady, I guess you're serious about
goin' to Columbia's School of Journalism."

"Of course, I've already got my application and
personal statement done."

"Ah-ight, ah-ight, I hear that, I hear that, you on
the case. You got your recommendations?"

"I don't have them yet, but I already have the
teachers lined up."

"Good, that's really good but back to the article,
and I admit that's a damn good article, but it's still not
clear to me what rioting accomplishes. I mean I understand
the feelin'. Believe me, when that Rodney King shit came
down, I definitely wanted to crack a cracker, but when you
look at what we get or don't get out of it, I mean you have
to wonder if it's worth it. I know you're not into rap, but
by any chance did you hear Paris' tape?"

"No, I can't say that I have."

"He's got a part on there talkin' about just that.
Uh'm, what's that jam? What's that jam? Uh'm, 'Long Hot
Summer'. Well, anyway, on the record, one of his boyz,
calls him durin' the riotin' in Cali, and they talk about the
same thing happenin' in 64' in Watts, and that the
community really didn't get anything out of that. Not too
long ago, I saw a picture in the New York Times where
there was a groundbreakin' ceremony in Newark's Central
Ward for a new $5 million Loews Newark Sixplex Theater,
scheduled to open last December. It stands on the spot
where the riots began in 1967, and except for a two-year-
old supermarket, is the only major business to open in the
central ward in twenty-five years! The second major
business to open in the central ward in twenty-five years!

Now what do you think is going to happen in South Central!"

"Oh, wow! That's truly messed up."

"It damn sure is." (Whether as the rioters or their immediate victims, it seems that black folk have ultimately and invariably paid a high price for American urban insurrections. In the long hot summer of July 1863 a draft riot in New York turned into a lynching party. Brothas and sistas were murdered on the streets. Many were forced to hide in Central Park or in New Jersey. Eyewitnesses to the massacre reported that a three year old child was hurled four stories to its death. A young mother who had given birth less than an hour before was set upon and pummeled while protectively clutching her baby! Babies were torn from their mother's arms and shot dead right in the mother's face. Brothas were literally torched. The riot was only halted by force of battalions called in from Gettysburg.)

Chapter Seven

In 1863, New York City may have been saved by the arrival of troops from Gettysburg, but as Freeman and O.K. stood along Hunter's third floor walkway chewing the fat and allowing their lunch to digest they had to wonder who was going to save the City in 1993.

"Look at that fat *DunkinDonuteatin'* cop down there, O.K.. I mean now damn, that fat pig is supposed to be a cop?"

"You hate cops don't you, Freeman?"

"Nah, how Ah'm a hate cops, my uncle's a cop."

Freeman's uncle, Tom, and his father were so unalike that it was hard to believe they had grown up in the same household. In fact, Freeman's father used to say that while he had outgrown the badges and incidences of slavery, his brother had grown out of them. Back in the '60s, while Freeman's father was helping organize SNCC chapters, his uncle was joining the Police Academy. Nothing in their upbringing would have led one to foresee that the two brothers' lives would take such radically divergent paths, but their lives were forever altered by the Harlem riots of 1964. High school students at the time, they both watched as their father's grocery store was looted. Freeman's father saw the riots as just part of the revolutionary tumult sweeping the nation as black people, tired of being second class citizens, weren't going to take it anymore. His older brother, Thomas, however, saw only his chances of going away to college, to Howard University, burn in the flames of the riot as his college money had to be used to rebuild their father's underinsured storefront. Although he was still able to go to college, and graduate, City College, his alma mater, would forever symbolize for him his broken dreams. No, Tom wasn't a revolutionary, he was a law and order man. An orderly law man. The two brothers spoke less often than Carter and Khohmeini. Well, actually, that was before Freeman's time, over the years they had settled into a sort of detente as Freeman's birth had moved the perennial bachelor, Tom, to reach out to Freeman's father. And when Freeman's mother died (while in Zimbabwe training nurses to attend to sick and injured guerrillas waging war against the colonial regime - she was a Panther till the end) Tom's interest in Freeman's welfare became even greater. Meanwhile, over the years Freeman's pops had come to appreciate the multifaceted dimensions of 'the struggle', as he referred to Black folk's confrontation with the American Dilemma. Still though, there was something about being a cop that he would never get past. It was kind of like how he'd refer to Colin Powell: "he was good, at a bad job."

"Yo', Freeman, you see homeboy over there?" O.K. said, as he pointed with his chin in the direction he wanted Freeman to look.

"Where?"

"Over there, outside the cafeteria."

"Yeah."

"How long he been at Hunter?"

"Phew, I don't know man, 7, 8 years. I remember when we were freshmen he was supposed to be a junior or something like that, but you know how that is." Freeman said while shaking his head in disgust and frustration.

"Yeah, I know, too many of us come here, and, I hate to say it, but it's true, bullshit, *youknowwhatah'msayin'*?"

"Yeah, I know. Sometimes you know though, even people who ain't bullshittin' get caught up in the system, and that fucks 'em up. I mean you come here, from some fuck'd up New York City public school, your math and readin' skills all underdeveloped, then they give you that test, and if you don't do well you've got to take all those remedial math and English classes before you even get to Math 120 or English 120, and then those remedial classes ain't worth nothing but one credit each toward graduatin', even though they count as full courses for financial aid purposes, and so the next thing you know, a semester has passed by and you look up and you've got four, count em, four credits!"

"So, what are you sayin', you think they should get full credit for remedial classes?"

"Man, Ah'm just sayin' it's a bad situation."

"So, yo', Freeman, how do you like tutorin'?"

"It's all right, it's better than my last job. Yo', remember when I was workin' part-time at that telephone marketin' job I got through the placement office? I was callin' people up tryin' to sell them magazines. Well we were dialin' by zip code, right, targetin' mostly white middle-class neighborhoods in Brooklyn and Queens. Now Ah'm doin' my job, Ah'm doin' my job, right, jus' doin' my job . . ."

"Yeah, yeah, Freeman, just doin' your job, and?"

"I was doin' my job, makin' my sales, callin' people up, when, and I'll never forget this shit, the fat ass white supervisor calls me into his office and says: 'Freeman, you're a smart guy, you wanna make it in the business world, don't you? I know you do. Well let me give you a piece of advice, if you're going to be successful in corporate America then you have to adapt to corporate America. The way you walk, the way you talk have to be more corporate. I've been listening to your calls and you have to watch your pronunciation. For example, it's not 'joynen' it's join-ing.' That fat bastard probably didn't even graduate from high school, couldn't say anything about my results, so he's tryin' to say my speech is too Black. I tell you, O.K., sometimes I just don't know."

"Yeah, I know what you mean, but that still doesn't tell me how you like tutorin'."

"Like I said, it's all right I get paid more than the library, I don't have to leave school, and I get to meet babes. What about you?"

"Yeah, it's ah-ight I guess, but no babes, you know how Black folk be runnin' from calculus."

"True indeed. I think it's 'cause we be confusin' the last two syllables wit' *Ku Klux, youknowwhatah'msayin'*." A laughing Freeman said.

"Boy, you crazy, you know that?"

"Yep. But seriously though, sometimes tutorin' can be snaps. I mean you have to laugh to keep from cryin'. I swear man, I've seen some brothas add the phrase, "and shit," to the end of their sentences."

"Stop, lyin'"

"Ah'm not lyin' man," Freeman chuckled, "even though a part of me wishes I was. I'm tellin' you, I've seen essays where the sentence will be like: 'I went to the store yesterday, and shit.'"

"Come on now, you bullshittin'," O.K. cried as he doubled over in laughter.

"Ah'm dead serious," a smiling Freeman replied.

"Well that just shows we've got a lot of work to do because the public schools obviously aren't gettin' the job done."

"I hear that, O.K., I hear that."

"So, wussup? What are we gonna do now?"

"Well I wanted to go check out Prof. Clarke."

"What's he talkin' about?"

"He's speakin' on his latest book 'African World Revolution'."

"Cool, let's go."

"I'm waitin' on Angelita."

"Hold up, now, she's comin'?! Tryin' to put her up on some Afrocentric shit, hanh?" O.K. said as he winked his left eye at Freeman, while simultaneously making a clicking sound with his mouth signifying his appreciation of Freeman's efforts with Angelita.

"Yeah, it's bugged out man. Before I started dealin' wit' her, I just thought they were intentionally denyin' their African roots. After bein' wit' her, though, I get the impression that they just think they started out in Panama or Puerto Rico or the Dominican Republic, as if they were always there. I don't know, sometimes I'm actually concerned that I might be negatively influencin' her wit' my North American prejudices."

"Oh as if they don't have biases against black people in Latin America. It ain't nothing but a pigmentocracy."

"Yeah, I know, man, but when you get right up on it, it's a little more complicated. Oh here she comes now. Hey what's up, Angelita?"

"What's up wit' you? Hi, O.K.."

"Hi. Me and your man were just havin' this deep conversation."

"Oh really, about what?"

"Race and self-concept?"

"Oh, yeah, so continue."

"Well, Freeman was just sayin' that sometimes he's afraid he's negatively influencin' you wit' his prejudices, but I was sayin' it ain't like you Latinos ain't already got some fuck'd prejudices your damn selves."

"Well," Angelita said, "the way I see it, some Blacks are racist against Latinos. I remember my first boyfriend was this light skin Dominican guy, he kinda looked like an Italian with a tan, and when we would go to the movies the Black guys would stare at us, and say things as we walked by."

"Well, Freeman, interjected, "I think that a lot of it has to do with language and meanings. I think African-Americans have a different conception of race and what they mean when they use the term 'race' than Latinos do. I mean when a Puerto Rican or Dominican uses Puerto Rican or Dominican as a racial description you lose me, cause those are national descriptions as far as Ah'm concerned, not racial. Like when Mellow Man Ace says "I'm not black, white nor Puerto Rican, just a stoopid Cuban." No, he's black and he's Cuban!"

(If Mellow Man Ace has any doubts he should look at what happened to Mario Baeza, when Clinton was set to name him undersecretary of state for Latin American affairs. Had he been appointed, Baeza would have held the most powerful Latin-American policymaking position in Washington, which would have made him the highest-ranking Cuban ever in the federal government. Instead of supporting him, however, those Spanish anti-Castro Miami lobbyists exploded in opposition, claiming that Baeza was not anti-Castro enough. These wealthy, conservative Cuban leaders, virtually stamped him an aider and abettor to Castro, just because he'd visited Cuba twice - once as a representative of the National Hispanic Bar Association and another time as the head of his law firm's Latin American Group. Both times he was in Cuba, he snuck off to see family he hadn't seen in years. And for this those Cuban leaders down in Miami claimed he couldn't be forgiven. Then these mostly Republican lobbyist, convinced wee-Bill wah-Bill Clinton to dump Baeza, despite the fact that Baeza was backed by Vernon Jordan and Ron Brown. Moreover, when Baeza's nomination was about to be blown up, the Congressional Black Caucus rose in his defense, and some of them said that they saw racism at work. Charles Rangel, whose mother is Puerto Rican, said that the lone distinction he saw between Baeza and the Cuban leaders in Miami opposing his selection, was his color. Rangel added that as far as he was concerned, it was a tragedy that American policies toward all of Latin America be determined by a handful of anti-Castro extremists. On the last point, Jose Serrano, the Puerto Rican congressman from the South Bronx and the head of the Congressional Hispanic Caucus, agreed with Rangel that it was foolish for America's foreign policy for all of Latin America to be determined by the political mood of South Florida.)

"Now, I think the confusion comes in," Freeman continued, "because Mellow Man Ace uses Black to mean African-American, ethnically, and we think he's denyin' his African background and react against that. It's kinda like when Jamaicans say "I'm not Black," they're usin' "Black" as shorthand for African-American, again an ethnic, not a racial comment," Freeman concluded.

"Well, yeah, all that's true," O.K. said, "but it's also that Black Americans are on the bottom, and you know, everybody associates us with crime, drugs, poverty, and the rest and so part of it is their reaction against bein' lumped in with a group that has such negative connotations."

"Oh, most definitely," Freeman agreed, "but with Latinos I think it is in fact more complex. I mean what Angelita said about her experience with her first boyfriend, Latinos are more mixed than us. While the slave-master took advantage of the situation to have his way with slave women in both English speakin' as well as Spanish speakin' America, in the Spanish speakin' part, there was much more intermarriage, and general intermixin' of the people, to the point where some of them, you know, just can't be described as being black or white, and then you throw in the Indian element. I mean, I've seen Puerto Rican families where the brother will look like Bobby Bonilla, and his sister will look like Lisette Menendez, *youknowwhatI'msayin'*."

"True, I remember this Puerto Rican girl I went to high school wit', homegirl had blond hair and blue eyes, but she had a straight up afro, that shit used to bug me out!"

"Yo', but you know what else, they be tryin' to pass."

"Tryin' to pass?!" Angelita said with a hint of anger.

"I mean not trying to pass for white," Freeman tippy toed, "but for anything other than bein' of African descent. I remember this Dominican girl tellin' me how people be mistakin' her for East Indian. I have to say she does look like one, a very dark one, but from my standpoint, if I wanted to be sensitive about the issue let's say, it was like she was happy that no one would think that she was black, *youknowwhatI'msayin'*, but then on the other hand, you've got people like Mario, you know, he's like that Santeria priest down in Miami, he looks more Spanish, but he's down wit' the Yoruba."

"We'll that's not just Latinos," Angelita said. "What about 'School Daze'?"

"Oh, don't get me wrong, I'm not sayin' it's just Latinos," Freeman responded. "In Derrick Bell's latest book, 'Faces at the Bottom of the Well', he writes of his own experiences growin' up. And explains how as a youngster he used to in effect brag that he was of Choctaw and Blackfoot Indian descent, deemphasizin' those Africans that came over on the slave ships. That's not to say that we should deny our Indian heritage, but we shouldn't embrace it as a means of denyin' our Africaness either. And I am sayin' that Latinos are more likely, to deny their personal African heritage than African-Americans are. What's that famous Puerto Rican poem you were tellin' me about? About hidin' your grandmother in the back because she was Black."

" 'Y Tu Aguela y A'onde Ejta?', by Fortunato Vizcarrondos."

"Like your homegirl Nilsa said, when she was younger her aunts and cousins would tell her sister that she

was prettier than Nilsa because she had straight hair, while
Nilsa's was curly."

Chapter Eight

"Yo', if a sista's hair is destined to go back to its
natural state, why do they call it a perm, after all it's only
temporary?"

"Yo', O.K. why you always gotta be callin' me wit'
these late night questions?" Freeman asked, as he rubbed
his eyes with the thumb and forefinger of his left hand,
while holding the phone in his right hand. He had been
sleeping, and he was trying to clear his head. "That's a
good question though I have to admit, but you still haven't
answered my question from this afternoon, are you goin'
to do the music at the Black Solidarity Day party or what?"

"Ya'll kickin' up the ducats?" O.K. asked, his
voice rising to show the necessity of his getting paid.

"Yeah, we got the ducats." Freeman offered.

"No, no, see Freeman I didn't ask if ya'll had them,
I asked were ya'll kickin' them up."

"Now, see, wit' that kind of analytical ability you
should be goin' to law school wit' me, I'm tellin' you." He
kidded O.K..

"Nah, not the kid, I'm like Sherry, it's strictly
business school for me. See, that way when my record
company starts comin' off I won't have to depend on no
white boy to run my shit."

"I hear you, I hear you, just be sure that I get your
legal work."

"Oh, you know dat, but first, you got's ta get
Angelita to hook me up wit' Nilsa."

"Oh, no, that again."

"Yes, that again."

"Why? I thought you was kickin' it to Jenne'?"

"What do you mean "why?", did I ask what was up wit' Sherry when you started kickin' it wit' Angelita?" O.K. countered, reminding Freeman of his own juggling act, "cause she's fine as the shits, and because I needs me a Latina babe to help me complete this jam I got's in my head."

"You crazy, I got's to give you that, you crazy." A laughing Freeman said.

"No, Ah'm serious."

"Yeah, seriously crazy. So, what are you sayin' that you want to rap in Spanish now?"

"Nah, but I am sayin' that we needs to incorporate some Latino shit into our shit. Look, check it out, if you look back in the day, some Puerto Ricans were on some dope jams. Remember that jam "Rockin' It" by the Fearless Four? They had that kid, uh'm, uh'm, Tito on it. In 1981, Mean Machine dropped "Disco Dreams," the first hip hop jam to use Spanish lyrics. And now look, I mean Mellow Man Ace's shit, "Mentirosa" sold over 750,000 copies in the U.S., and went to as high as No. 14 on Billboard's Hot 100."

"Get outta here!" Freeman remembered the record being popular, but he hadn't realized *how* popular.

"Straight up. Shit, "La Raza", by Kid Frost, charted on the Hot Rap Singles chart, while his album, 'Hispanic Causing Panic' charted on the Top Pop Album and Top Black Album charts."

"For real?!" He was growing more intrigued about the prospects for the convergence of African-American and Latino musical culture.

"Yes! Look at how that Puerto Rican kid, Fat Joe, is comin' off."

"Yeah, but he's not rappin' in Spanish."

"Nevertheless, that's besides the point, the fact remains. I mean look at the neighborhood, Negro's and Puerto Ricans been rollin' in the same places for as long as I can remember, something had to rub off both ways. You got to tap that market. Look, remember KRS-ONE made that salsafied version of "I'm Still No. 1"?"

"Wasn't that "My Philosophy"?"

"Whatever, I'm not sure, but the point remains the same. Check it, Nice & Smooth made that bilingual jam "Hip Hop Junkies." Shit, even 2 Live Crew made a bilingual jam, what is it, hold on a sec, I've got it right here . . ."

"You got a 2 Live Crew jam?"

"I'm tryin' to get up on the bilingual shit. Oh here it is, "Mamolapenga". They used some Santana shit to put this one together."

"Damn, you serious."

"*T h a t ' s w h a t a h ' m t r y i n ' t o t e l l u !* *That'swhyuneedtahavethat PuertoRicanchick . . .*"

"Dominican"

". . . *putusuponsomeSalsajams.* Shit, the shit is all African. Here check out this article I clipped out of the Daily News. It's about Mario Bauza, the Cuban trumpeter. He was performin' in Newark at a show entitled a "Latin Jazz Dance Party," Bauza says his music is the synthesis of Cuba and Africa."

"Yeah, ah-ight. I'll bring it up next time I see her."

"When is that going to be?"

"I'm supposed to be going to her house for dinner, to meet her family, and shit."

"Damn. You, better get used to rice and beans."

"Come on."

"All right, all right, but can I ask you something?"

"Go head."

"Have you tapped that yet?"

"Tapped what yet?"

"Why you always gotta be so difficult you know what I'm talkin' about. Have you knocked those boots yet?"

"N-O-PE."

"Damn! You killin' me, here I am tryin' to live vicariously, and shit, and you messin' up shop. Damn, I know that would be some good shit!"

"And how do you know that pray-tell?"

"Cauz them Latin babes iz hot! Take one up to Mount Everest and you'll cause a flood from the snow they'll melt."

"And what makes 'em so hot?"

"Yo', I don't know, I guess it's the food, all those spices, rice and beans and plantains, and shit, especially those plátanos."

"You crazy! You are crazy!"

"Nah, mań, Ah'm serious, I mean check it, compare it to American Negro food, you know collard greens . . ."

"Collard greens?!" Said Freeman, his voice deepening and suggesting a distaste for the Southern staple, but O.K. called him on it.

"Don't even front, Negro, both DMC and Snoop Doggy Dogg gave much praise to collard greens on two different coasts almost a decade apart, so you know Negroes' iz eatin' collard greens, so will you let me continue please?"

"Continue."

"Collard greens! . . ."

Chapter Nine

As Freeman sat at Angelita's table to dine, he had one question on his mind.

"Yo', Angelita, why didn't you tell me that your brother was married to a white girl?" He whispered.

"Well, it's a long story. You know he's a cop, and that he's in the National Guard, right? Well durin' the Gulf War he got called up to serve in Saudi Arabia. While he was there, he saw this ad in Stars and Stripes, the Army magazine, about Russian women lookin' for American men to marry. The magazine had pictures of the women, and I don't know, I guess he liked the way they looked. He knew my mother would like it, you know them bein' white and all. After all, she is always talkin' about improvin' the race. Well anyway, he wrote to this matchmakin' company and the rest, is, as you say, history."

"Yo', you mean he got wit' her, kind of like, through the mail?" A dumbfounded Freeman asked, his frowning face reflecting his confusion, and his confusion confirmed by his twin open palms jutting upward with each quizzical word.

"You could say that."

"Yo', that's bugged!" (Being more interested in what his father called the 'First World', that is the 'Black World', Freeman was unaware that an unexpected side-effect of the defrosting of the Eastern bloc has been the creation of a booming business in Russian snow bunnies eager to leave the sagging economy of the Commonwealth of Independent States for the gold-laden streets of America. In December 1990, The Chicago Tribune reported that for $25, an American male could buy a package of a dozen photos of and letters from eligible and willing Russian women from American-Russian Matchmaking, a company based in Los Angeles.

In April 1990, a Russian computer software designer turned entrepreneur, Sergei Kurockkin founded Nahodka, a trans-Atlantic matchmaking firm. In English Nahodka means Godsend, and those involved in the international matchmaking business, hoped that the new Russian women would be just that.)

"So, how'd you meet your wife, Olga?" Freeman asked. Angelita gave him a subtle, but effective disapproving glance, but "Ralph," as her brother Rafael liked to be called, was happy to discuss it, after all, as far as he was concerned, he had struck gold, Russian gold.

"Well, while I was stationed in Saudi Arabia, during Operation Desert Storm, I came across this ad in Stars and Stripes magazine, by this company, Nahodka, which in English means, Godsend, and believe me that's precisely what it was for me, well, anyway this ad was looking for American men who were interested in meeting Russian women, for possible matrimony." As Ralph spoke, Freeman couldn't help but marvel at how much he sounded like a whiteboy, one of those Long Island whiteboys he must work with down at the station, Freeman thought, but then again, he thought it was too formal and rigid, Ralph sounded like someone who was trying to effect an intelligent air, Freeman decided. "Well, this ad," Ralph continued, "had a picture of Olga in it, and I knew right away she was going to be my wife. I wrote Nahodka, and became a client. Soon I was corresponding with Olga by mail. After the successful campaign in the desert, I returned to the States and arranged through the company to visit the former Soviet Union for ten days to get to better know my prospective bride. The trip cost me almost

$3,000, and the actual marriage, another $3,000, ate up most of my savings, but it was well worth it.

"When we met, it was love at first sight." Freeman wondered how that could be. "'Love at first sight'?" He asked himself. Olga was a pale brunette, with a round Slavic face suggesting some Asian ancestry, which gave her eyes an almost almond shape and helped to soften her otherwise stoic features; nevertheless, Freeman could see that she was a little on the plump side. And, moreover, she spoke in monotonous, monosyllabic, halting English. He knew it would have driven him crazy, but not Ralph, who continued to extol the virtues of their relationship. "I immediately arranged for a fiancee visa which gave us ninety days to marry before Olga would have had to leave the country."

"How do you get a fiancee visa?" Freeman asked. Again, Angelita gave him a disapproving look, she knew him well enough to know that he was mocking her brother.

"Well, the couple must have already met. If not, you could get a six-month visitor's visa which would only have required that Olga have had an invitation from me. She would have needed convincing evidence that she intended to return to Russia, though, and we were much too in love to have been able to pull that one off. We were married ten days after she arrived."

(Actually, it was amazing that it had taken that long. In the sagging Russian economy, Olga had been unemployed for seventeen months prior to hearing from Ralph, and unbeknownst to him, she had turned on her back to make ends meet. When Ralph's letters started pouring in, it was she thought, a Godsend. When she first saw Ralph, she was disappointed that he was not the Tom Cruise look-alike she had prayed for; instead, Ralph looked more like the offspring Diana Ross and Julio Iglesias would produce if they got together. Not having yet gone through the American initiation into whiteness, however, she was not completely opposed to marrying him. Besides, the man really didn't matter, his passport did.

Since the fall of the Soviet Union, Russian immigration policies have been made less rigid, and Russian women have become a major part of the international matchmaking business. In 1992, one company alone, Scanna International handled nearly 5,000 American men seeking Russian wives, while the company itself had listings for nearly 20,000 Russian women. It was a buyer's market.

Companies that at one time were primarily involved in the Asian mail-order bride business have shifted their focus to Russia. Numerous companies have opened in the former Soviet Union itself, running ads in newspapers from The Russian Daily to The Village Voice. Scanna itself regularly publishes a biweekly register it sells for $5 and includes biographies and photos of two hundred new women -- addresses go for $10 -- actually, only $7 if the gentleman purchases at least ten.

Had Freeman known more about this interesting sidebar to the end of the Cold War, he would have seen that the global racial hierarchy that Malcolm described as White World Supremacy even manifests itself in the international matchmaking business. While Russian women are in demand, and Asian women are acceptable, secondarily, as marriage partners, Dominican women, are a major element of the global market in prostitution. Driven in large part by severe economic crisis, prostitution in the Dominican Republic capital of Santo Domingo has exploded. According to a New York Times report, in the city of nearly two million, there are no less than 20,000 prostitutes the vast majority of whom are young women, between the ages of sixteen and twenty-five. The sex trade also includes many men who indulge the sexual fantasies of both sexes. Many younger girls also find themselves pushed into the trade out of economic pressure. It's estimated that there may be as many 60,000 prostitutes in the country. The Dominican Republic's national reputation has been sullied by the belief that it is such a prodigious source for the sex trade from the Netherlands to Haiti, and diverse countries in between. According to one estimate, on the tiny island of Antigua, there are 4,000 Dominican prostitutes out of a total population of 80,000, while another 7,000 Dominicans are estimated to work in the Amsterdam sex industry.)

"So what do you think about the controversy in the Hispanic Society about whether to back Dinkins or Giuliani?" Freeman asked Ralph, marvelling at what he would come up with next.

"Well, first, I refuse to join the Hispanic Society," Ralph said with an air of righteous indignation, "that kind of stuff only creates division, it's a form of separation. We don't see race in the police department. There are no Dominicans, Italians, Irish, Jews, Puerto Ricans or Blacks. The only color we see is blue. You could say we're boys in the 'hood, the police brotherhood. My heart goes out to that cop who had that bucket dropped on him."

"Yeah, that was terrible," Freeman agreed, before Ralph continued, "these black and Spanish guys who want to form their own organizations within the police department are only stirring up trouble. You don't see white guys forming separate organizations," Ralph said, pausing for effect, to let his point sink in, before glancing at his mother who was beaming proudly, and smiling approvingly. (Actually, contrary to Ralph's contentions, and despite his mother's support of his views, the police department, depending on one's view, is either one of the great proponents of diversity or a hotbed of intense ethnic competition, as witnessed by the bevy of organizations representing European ethnic as well as Black and Latino cops. There's the Emerald Society, an organization representing the city's Irish-American police officers. There is also the 6,000-member Columbia Society, an Italian-American fraternal organization, which since its inception in 1930 had not endorsed any political candidate, only to break with that tradition by backing Giuliani in the 1989 mayoral campaign. And there is also the Shorim Society, an association of Jewish officers. Mayor Dinkins was the first person to win the city's mayoralty without winning a majority of either of the Italian, the Irish or the Jewish vote. He did it by winning nine out of ten Black votes and two out of every three Latino voters. (Ralph, was in the one-third minority. He voted his color: blue, and backed Giuliani.) Dinkins was backed by the black fraternal police organization, the Guardians Association while the Hispanic Society, contrary to popular opinion in the Latino community, backed Mr. Giuliani.) "I'm telling you Freeman," Ralph continued, "in the police house, there are no such divisions, we're all just one big family. As a matter of fact, I'm having a cookout at my house tomorrow for some of my buddies from the force, you're welcome to come if you want."

        "No, thanks for offering though, but I really have to study for exams." Freeman couldn't believe this guy, "Angelita certainly must not have told her brother about my editorials," he said to himself, "invitin' me to a police cookout?! Was he tryin' to get a brotha lynched?!" Her brother really was lost, Freeman thought. "It's a damn shame," he said under his breath. 'Just one big family', he

repeated in his disbelieving mind. He was convinced Ralph
was in for a rude awakening.

"Enough you two," Angelita said, "let's eat. I think
you're going to love this Freeman, this is one of my
favorite dishes, Piononos."

"Pi . . . Pi . . ."

"Piononos"

"Pionones?"

"Hmmph, almost, Piononos."

"Piononos."

"Esta bien."

"What is it?"

"Stuffed plantains."

"Stuffed plantains? Hmmph, how do you make it?"

"Okay, well, first you slice the plantains the long
way, three or four strips depending on how thick the
plantain is, then you lightly fry the slices until they're
golden. Use a paper towel to drain off excess oil. Then you
pour achiote oil into the pan and brown the beef, remember
only fry it until it's browned, not till it's crisp, and be sure
to break it up so no lumps are formed. Okay then you can
add garlic, bell pepper, and scallions. Make sure you stir
it thoroughly. Then add ham . . .

"Excuse me?"

"Ahem, well, we know you're not going to use any
ham, or as you say swine! But Dominicans would add ham,
you can do without the ham. So, skip the ham, add
cornstarch, tomatoes, capers, and tamarind. Then lastly,
add some salt, pepper, and chilli pepper. Stir all of this in
a few tablespoons of water and heat it on a low flame for
about four minutes, until it's got some body and the flavors
blend in. Then heat the achiote for deep frying. Fold each
slice into a circle, then stuff them with the mixture, stuff
it in firmly and smooth the top so that you'll have pretty

firm patties. In the meantime, beat some eggs in a wide, shallow bowl, then dip each patty into the egg batter, make sure that they're completely covered with the batter, and then drop them into the simmering oil, and brown them some more, for about four minutes, and then drain them on paper towels. And presto, you're ready to get your eat on."

"You know, Angelita, I didn't need the blow by blow, all you had to say was fried plantains stuffed with beef."

"Oh but it's so much more than that, and besides you have to learn how to cook!"

While Angelita's eyes glistened brightly as she spoke to Freeman, her mother's burned with thinly veiled contempt. Like every other immigrant she had been bombarded by negative images of African-Americans blasted daily on the television, on the radio, in the newspapers and magazines. She, herself, had had a gold chain snatched by a young brotha during the chain snatching craze of the early eighties. And that experience, coupled with the negative views and images ubiquitously dispersed throughout the media, reinforced the negative connotations associated with blackness that she learned growing up in the DR. In many ways, Samaná, was a product of her environment. She had simply absorbed the views of the Dominican dominant classes who continue to deify the nation's Spanish and Catholic past, while simultaneously attempting to sweep under the rug the nation's African heritage. In an article in Newsday, District 6 community school board member, Anthony Stevens-Acevedo, recalled how for decades in the Dominican Republic when Dominicans got their national ID cards if they were visibly of African descent they would be classified as "Indian." And when at sixteen he went for his ID card the clerk wrote that he was Indian. Acevedo objected and told the clerk, "I'm Black," but the clerk told him, that it wasn't in his best interest to say he was black, it would be better to say Indian. Now, as she looked at Freeman, Angelita's mom was awash in guilt, she felt that she had somehow failed her daughter. "Why couldn't she be like her brother?" She asked herself, wondering where she had gone wrong?" Her daughter was making a terrible mistake, and she was not going to stand back and just let it happen, as soon as dinner was over she was going to tell her daughter how it was.

Chapter Ten

"You're so young, you don't understand Angelita, you have to think ahead, to improve the race."

"Think ahead; improve the race?! What kind of talk is that Mami, look at abuela."

"And that is why she married your grandfather, to improve her line."

"You know Mami, you're so blind you don't even see it. When I think of all the times you used to tell me how you would rub your milk on my head when I was a baby, so that I would have good hair. What are you saying, Mami? Yes. My hair is straight, even though it's kinda wavy, but look it's black-black. Would you rather it was blond? Would you rather the full lips I got from abuela were thin like them white girls you look at in the magazines? Would you rather my skin was lighter? I bet you would. "Stay out of the sun, you don't want to look like Haitians," remember that Mami, don't you see, our ancestors didn't just come from Spain, we are not Conquistadors. Our ancestors came here just like the Blacks you look down on, like the Haitians you hate. In the hulls of ships, dragged off from their homelands. You

know what they say, Mami, every Dominican has a little
black behind the ears, you know, "todos los Dominicanos
tienen el negro detras de las orejas." We are more like the
Haitians than the Castilians. Look at what our Presidente
did, spending all of that money foolishly to celebrate the
500th anniversary of Columbus. And you, abuela, I mean
really, using the Santos to keep me and Freeman apart."

"You don't understand Angelita, look at your
sister."

"I'm not her, Mami!" Angelita yelled back, fighting
back her tears. Angelita's sister, Peaches (She was so
nicknamed for her fondness of the fruit of the same name
as a little girl, and for those who didn't know her as a little
girl for the small tattoo of peaches she had on her left
ankle.) had, to her mother's eternal damnation, gotten
pregnant in high school. The first time Freeman saw
Peaches she was the picture of subtlety. He and Angelita
had just gotten back from taking Peaches' son Miguel to
the movies, and Peaches had come to Angelita's to pick
him up. She was dressed in a peach colored sweater with
a peach colored leather jacket, he could see that she also
had on peach colored socks, as well as freshly painted
peach colored nails- she'd just had painted at a Korean
owned nail salon. He wondered what color her underwear
were. Really. Her hair had peach highlights, her earrings -
peaches, and she also had two small gold chains. One said
Peaches, and one had two small gold peaches attached to
it. She was indeed the master of understatement, he
thought. He'd never forget her first words, "Jo' Angelita
Ah'm not votin'." "But, why?" Her sister had asked, not
really expecting a cogent answer, but wanting to hear what
she had to say anyway. "'Cauz, jo', Dinkins ain't did
nothin' for me, and 'cauz I don't trust Giuliani, he's
prejudiced against Dominicans."

Chapter Eleven

While Angelita and her mother argued, Freeman was strolling down the block from Angelita's house to the train station. Before he got to the train, however, he was transfixed and mesmerized as he walked past a bevy of décolleté dress wearing beauties, silver and gold crosses sparkling against their enticing breasts, standing on line waiting to get into Club 2000, a premiere Washington Heights Hip-Hop and Merengue club. You could tell those who grew up in New York from those who'd just arrived by which night they attended and how they dressed. By the way the women were dressed, much too formal for Hip Hop, Freeman concluded it was a Meringue night and dismissed any fleeting notion of checking it out. As he looked back to catch a final glimpse of a woman who'd given him the eye, he was struck by a red neon cross shining further up the block and to the right. The cross-shaped beam could be seen all the way across the street, and to Freeman it seemed a miniature version of the Columbus lighthouse he'd read about in his Latin American politics course. (The *faro a Colon* was originally trumpeted by the Dominican government as a colossal tourist attraction. Its completion was timed to coincide with 1992's quincentennial celebration in the hopes that it would attract millions of foreign tourists and much needed foreign currency. Its thirty billion-candle power lights are alleged to be able to radiate cross-shaped beams through the night sky capable of being seen as far away as Puerto Rico, 150 miles to the east. The Lighthouse's supporters argue that the 10-story high, cross-shaped, cement, half-mile long mausoleum will prove an important legacy for future generations. They argue that its Pharaonic proportions will bring Santo Domingo like fame as Pharos island in the bay of Alexandria, Egypt known for its magnificent lighthouse. And contend that like the lighthouse in Pharos, the Dominican lighthouse will become a profit producing tourist magnet, drawing both foreign visitors and Dominicans, to its historical exhibits organized around the theme of Europe's discovery of the Americas. The project's critics point to its tremendous cost, estimated at $70 million, and the immorality implicit in glorifying the man whose colonization of Hispaniola rapidly resulted in the extermination of the island's Indian population. Moreover, they condemn President Balaguer's glorification of the country's Spanish heritage, while denying the contributions of Africans and their descendants, who make up the overwhelming majority of the country's population.

Some of those descendants residing in the Maquiteria ghetto at Santo Domingo's eastern edge (where much of Angelita's extended family still lived) found that many of their homes were destroyed to make room for this second coming of Columbus. And now when the lighthouse shines its light, their lights dim and their television pictures shrink.)

As he saddled up to the iron horse, and copped a squat for the long ride home, Freeman took a swig of the Guanabana nectar he'd just bought to quench his thirst, and opened up the Amsterdam News he'd just purchased to keep himself company during the long ride home. Flipping through the paper, his attention was soon captured by a review of Eddy L. Harris' book 'Native Stranger'. The reviewer must have known what Freeman had been thinking about moments before, because in the course of the review she compared Dominican President Balaguer to the President of the Ivory Coast, Houphoet-Boigny, asking rhetorically, what it was about certain leaders of non-European nations that would possess them to build monumental structures deifying European civilization? The reviewer was particularly outraged by Houphoet-Boigny's obstinance. In spite of the fact that the engine behind the Ivory Coast's economic expansion has run out of steam, as world market prices for coffee and cocoa have plummeted. And in spite of the fact that unemployment has skyrocketed, and health-care problems have ballooned. Despite those myriad mounting difficulties, Boigny continued to work hard to assure that Ivorians, like Dominicans would at least have a grand alabaster mastodon, a great white elephant dwelling in the midst of a colored nation. As described by Harris: "A great and monumental church, big and beautiful and lasting . . . a massive Catholic basilica [built] in the jungle of a nation of people the vast majority of whom are animist."

(Upon completion, this colossal basilica, became the largest Christian church in the world, dwarfing even Saint Peter's Basilica in Rome. President Boigny claimed that the church's construction was being financed with family money.

'Our Lady of Peace' was constructed from marble imported from Italy. (After all, we can't use African resources now, come on, when you're going to go colonial you might as well go all the way.) At a cost of over $250 million, this elephantine colossus was worked on for three years, and after numerous *twentyfourseven* weeks of labor, was finally completed. When the fat lady finally sang there were two acres of stained glass windows. Two hundred seventy-two columns supported the mighty pachyderm. And from the tip of the cross at the top of the dome to the ground below, the church stood 489 feet high. And although only one in five in this nation of ten million is Christian, the Church's esplanade has enough room for more than eighteen thousand worshipers. [Isn't that just like a Negro, go out and buy a mansion, before he can afford a co-op?]

Houphouet-Boigny claimed the church was a monument to his people. The reviewer, however, swore that as dusk dawned the basilica cast a shadow eerily reminiscent of the President's own.)

One day before the quincentenary celebration of Columbus' invasion of the Americas, Angelita's mother and grandmother, who viewing themselves as devout Catholics and good Dominican citizens had flown down for the celebration, were among the huge throng of Dominican worshipers and church leaders from throughout Latin America who celebrated Mass at the foot of The Lighthouse with Pope John Paul II. Confronted with protest against the glorification of Columbus, the Pope was repeatedly forced to assert that the Mass was meant to commemorate the evangelization of the Americas, not their colonization. In New York, Cardinal O'Connor, made the same argument in response to criticism over the Church's participation in the Columbus Day parade. He also praised the missionaries accompanying Columbus for recognizing the humanity of the indigenous population, and their capacity to be saved (in a religious sense). As he turned the lock and entered his home, Freeman laughed to himself when he remembered his grandfather telling him: "When the white man arrived in Hawaii, the Hawaiians had the land, and the white man had the Bible, forty years later, the Hawaiians had the Bible, and the white man had the land."

Back in the Dominican Republic the Pope agreed to meet with delegates from Indian and black groups from throughout the hemisphere. He also met with a committee of conservative Haitian bishops. They asked him to support their call for the ending of the year-old hemisphere-wide embargo imposed on Haiti in an effort to defeat the military overthrow of Aristide. Aristide had sharply castigated the Pope the month before in a speech at the UN saying that of all the world's governments, the Vatican alone had officially blessed the coup.

Chapter Twelve

When Freeman got home from dinner he was still enjoying the memory of the piononos he'd been introduced to earlier that evening, and he gave Angelita a call to let her know that he'd gotten home and to get the recipe.

"Hey, what's up, Angelita, I just wanted to call you before I went to bed. Hey, what's wrong, you sound upset? What's wrong?"

"Nothing."

"It doesn't sound like nothing, tell me, what's wrong?"

"I just got into an argument with my mother."

"About what?"

"About you?"

"About me? Why me?"

"She doesn't want me seein' any Black guys."

"Angelita, might I point out that your grandmom's, your mother's mother, is like a couple of shades darker than me."

"I know, it's like we Dominicans say "we all have a little black behind the ears." Unfortunately, that's where most of us want to keep it, behind the ears."

"Damn, that's wild. Some of my older relatives tell me how when they were growin' up, if somebody called you black, those were fightin' words. Now I can't even imagine that shit, but hey, we makin' progress. It's on us, the first generation of decolonized minds. So let's not dwell on that, besides, I've got something that will cheer you up."

"What?"

"Well I only do this on special occasions, with special women," Freeman said playfully.

"Yeah, yeah, what?"

"Well, we're goin' to write a poem together right now over the phone, each line more intense than the last, so that by the time we finish you'll want to come runnin' over here and crawl into bed with me."

"My aren't we sure of ourselves."

"When you got it like I got it, you've got to be sure of yourself. You ready?"

"Yeah, Ah'm ready."

"Blazing cold against my lips."

" . . ."

"Uh' you're supposed to come up with the next line."

"I know I was just thinkin'."

"No, it doesn't work like dat baby, you got's to be spontaneous. Come on, now, again: Blazing cold against my lips."

"The icy snow flakes falling."

"That was good, that was good," Freeman said as he chuckled, enjoying Angelita's participation. "Okay, here we go again. Holdin' hands walkin' over fluffy snow."

"I hear his heartbeat callin'"

"Are you sure you've never done this before?" Freeman joked. "Okay, okay, but first let me put some Sade on in the background here 'cause you tryin' to outdo me, and I need some inspiration. Okay here we go: At the sight of her warm smile my soul doth shake."

"'My soul doth shake' come on Freeman, now, what are you in Old England." Angelita teased him.

"Yo', that's it, that shit is dope, 'At the sight of her warm smile, my soul doth shake'."

"Yeah, Freeman, whatever you say."

"Come on now, Angelita stop stallin': 'At the sight of her warm smile, my soul doth shake'."

"His every touch makes me shiver and quake."

"We taste the flakes in between kisses."

"And watch them melt from the heat that our bodies create."

"Sinkin' into her most sublime secrets, I'm warmed by her supple skin."

"Our bodies crushed together creates a fire within."

"Your breath ignites my passion, each sigh beckons irresistibly."

"As I feel his hands caressin' my thighs, I'm frozen by the thrill arisin' in me."

"She moans softly wrapping her softness around me."

"I feel his hands caressing me softly."

"We exist in bliss as her juice drenches me until our final passionate embrace when milk and honey mix as one."

Chapter Thirteen

After talking with Freeman, and drinking a cold bottle of Snapple lemonade to cool off, Angelita decided to give her cousin, Julia, a call. Julia, had just come up in the last year from the Dominican Republic, she worked in a beauty shop in Washington Heights. Being pretty much

straight from the D.R., Julia, still harbored many of her
native prejudices, as Angelita was about to find out.

"Does he have good hair or bad hair?" Was Julia's
first question.

"What do you mean good hair or bad hair?" An
agitated Angelita asked.

"You know hair like ours, good."

"And hair like grandma's?"

"Hair like grandma's? "

"Yes, hair like grandma's."

"That's bad."

"And what makes it bad?"

"Because, you know, hair like ours is easy to
manage. And girls with bad hair spend hours trying to get
their hair like ours. I tell you Angelita, just the other day,
I spent three hours working on this girl's hair. . ."

"Julia, grandma does not have bad hair, as a matter
of fact, there's no such thing as pelo malo. How can hair
be bad? Does it attack you? Is it mean? Does it enslave
people? No! It's not bad, it's just different. It's only
considered bad because the Spaniards put themselves on a
pedestal, and made us want to look like them. Yeah, our
hair is 'good' you say, but it's black-black, is blonde hair
better? What about your complexion, is white skin better?"
As Angelita finished talking to her cousin, she heard the
front door open and close, and the sounds of Fat Joe
booming through a walkman - she knew her younger
brother was home. She was angry with him for missing
dinner earlier, but she was glad he was home. Among all
of their family, Angelita and Pablo shared a special bond.
Their views and self-perception had been greatly influenced
by the confluence of Afrocentricity and Hip-Hop, and set
them apart from the rest of their family, except, maybe the
outcast - Peaches, well, at least the Hip-Hop part, anyway.

Chapter Fourteen

When Freeman got off the phone with Angelita, he was still tripping about her mother's attitude. He could hear his pops typing downstairs, and he went to talk to him about it. He figured he'd have some insight since he was at the moment writing a book about Black and Latino political coalitions in New York; in addition to working on the Dinkins' campaign.

"Well, Free, you've got to understand that in the Dominican Republic the Spanish quickly found themselves outnumbered by the descendants of all those Africans they'd imported, and by the revolutionary Haitians next door. And then when the Haitians took over! I mean, my goodness, the blacks were ruling! They had to do something. When you look at the three principal leaders of the Dominican revolt against Haitian rule: Juan Pablo Duarte, Ramon Mella and Francisco del Rosario Sanchez, they're all pretty much straight up Spaniards. According to the historian Juan Bosch, Dominican history has been systematically slanted to create the impression that the twenty-two years of Haitian rule were marked by barbaric oppression. But according to Bosch many Dominicans supported the takeover. After all, if you were enslaved, freedom had come. And even if you weren't, under the racial order the Spanish had imposed people of African descent were at the bottom, so they also welcomed a change in the racial pecking order.

"Now, take it to America. As I was explaining, about it being in the interest of the ruling class in the Dominican Republic to sell the masses this false notion of their whiteness, or at least their Indianess (as a sort of consolation prize if they so obviously weren't "white"), in order to ensure their support against the Haitians, so today are white Americans interested in driving a wedge between African-Americans and Latinos by playing to Latinos Spanish heritage above and beyond their indigenous and African heritage. Let me put a little theoretical construct on it for you. I was just reading this paper out of the University of Chicago, by Nancy Denton and Douglas Massey entitled 'Racial Segregation of Caribbean Hispanics'. These two sociologists contend, that in the United States, Latinos from the Caribbean are challenged by a profound confrontation between two clashing and contradictory delineations of race. In the Spanish speaking Caribbean, they point out that race is defined along a multicategory continuum, but in the U.S., it's bipolar - black or white. As a result, people from the Spanish speaking Caribbean face pressures to identify themselves as either black or white. Now obviously this creates a dilemma because in America, Race Matters - being black means being in the downtrodden class, while being white carries advantages.

"These professors point out that another potential source of pressure could arise from the nascent formation and evolution of a Latino ethnic grouping. Now before coming to the good ol' U.S. of A. most Latinos see themselves as just part of their national group, Puerto Rican, Mexican, Cuban, etcetera. In the U.S., though, they begin to develop an ethnic identity based on what they have in common. They all speak Spanish, for the most part they're Catholic, and they all have roots in Latin America, accordingly then, over time, a "Latino" ethnicity develops.

"So, if one follows this line of reasoning, then you would see that in the U.S. Latinos from the Caribbean are being pulled in opposite directions. On one hand, they are, as Massey and Denton say, united around their common identity as Latinos. On the other hand, they're split along racial lines as they conform to the rest of America's bipolar racial canon.

"In the last year the Atlantic Monthly has run two huge articles on the breakdown or the coming breakdown in relations between African-Americans and Latinos, one specifically on New York City: dealing with Blacks and Puerto Ricans, and one on LA: dealing with Blacks and Mexicans, now why do you think that is? When it's to white folks advantage they talk about the particular Latino group, be it Puerto Rican, Mexican, Cuban or what have you, but when it's not in their interest to so separate them, then they'll lump them together under the rubric "Hispanic." Case in point (In Ed Koch's commercial endorsing Herman Badillo, at one point he refers to the candidate as the first Hispanic, and at another point as the first Puerto Rican. And even the conservative Robert Novak predicting a defection of Latinos from Dinkins, wrote of blacks and nonblacks, an obvious inversion of the usual white and nonwhite delineation of American politics), I was reading this editorial in New York Newsday's New York Forum entitled 'The Coalition of Color Fades'. The white boy argues that the rift in the Black and Latino political alliance that voted Dinkins in is becoming more apparent every day. And to prove his point he cites Michael Woo's losing effort in the L.A. mayoral race. He writes that Woo lost, despite winning the overwhelming percentage of blacks votes because he barely won the Latino vote. He ignores the low black turnout, and the fact that Woo did indeed win the majority of black votes and the majority of Latino votes, as well, while he lost the white vote, overwhelmingly! He also points to the Houston mayoral race where Bob Lanier, a white businessman, defeated Sylvester Turner, a black lawyer, on the strength, according to the author, of a record turnout of Hispanic

voters. What he fails to point out, however, is that in both
of these cases the Hispanics he's talking about are
overwhelmingly Mexican. Therefore this may or may not
be relevant to the coalition between African-Americans and
Latinos from the Caribbean, in New York City. After all,
wasn't Bronx Borough President Fernando Ferrer quoted as
saying that the new schools chancellor Cortines had no
connection to New York's Latinos, that he didn't even
speak Spanish. Yet, this article seeks to suggest that
Dinkins' failure to back Cortines hurt black and Latino
relations in the City. You know what the beautiful thing
about America is though, Free?"

"No."

"The beautiful thing about America is - we're all in
the same boat, white folks don't care if you're one thirty-
second African or one hundred percent; for them, a nigger
is a nigger. So let your girlfriend's mother protest all she
wants, the forces of society dictate that the younger ones
will increasingly be drawn to see their connection with us,
and all of our connections with Africa."

As Freeman tossed and turned in his bed that night
he remembered an earlier phone conversation he'd had with
Pablo, Angelita's younger brother. He laughed when he
recalled Pablo's response when he asked him what he
thought of Fat Joe, whose album was at the moment
blowing up. He grinned and shook his head as he repeated
Pablo's response: "That nigga's dope!" "How bout that,"
he said to himself, "a Dominican, sounding like an
African-American, calling a Puerto Rican a nigga, as the
word is sometimes applied in the endearment mode. Yeah,
shit is funny sometimes," he said to himself, just before he
lost consciousness.

Chapter Fifteen

Getting to school via the subway was always an adventure for Freeman, and on occasion a dangerous one. He had to be on guard as he traveled a tortuous path from the Park Slope brownstone he, his younger brother, Earl, and his father shared. Transferring every morning from the D train to the 4 train at Atlantic Avenue, on his way to catching the 6 at Grand Central taking him to his ultimate destination, 68th Street - Hunter College. On this particular morning, Freeman was still angry about Angelita's mother. In his anger he forgot to mind his business and interrupted a robbery in process, only to find himself face to face with a menace to society.

"Oh! Oh! You wanna be a hero?! You know what we do to heroes? I'll show you what we do to heroes!" As the young buck's hand disappeared into his jacket in search of that power coming out of the barrel of a gun, Freeman was asking himself what had possessed him to dare to speak up. He'd grown up witnessing numerous vics, so it wasn't anything he hadn't seen before. Moreover, the would be jackers were exponentially growing more and more daring and violent everyday. It wasn't his fault after all. The brotha shouldn't have bought one of those fancy leather knapsacks, he should have stuck to good ol' canvass, but alas, he didn't and now Freeman was in the pot boiling along with him. "Damn!" He said to himself, "first semester of my last year in college, and I'm goin' to die over someonelse's knapsack!" It wasn't that he was afraid, so much as disappointed by the sheer senselessness of it all. If he were going to be killed, he wanted to die as the Last Poets had rapped long ago, for a cause, not because.

Not because Negroes had not only failed to heed the words of the Poet's classic, 'When the Revolution Comes', but had outright rejected them and confirmed and affirmed their propensity to "party and bullshit, and party and bullshit and party and bullshit," as rapped on the intensely funky jam of the same name from the 'Who's the Man?' soundtrack. Once again proving that not only are 'Niggers . . . Scared of Revolution', but in some cases are actually devolving, for as 'Party and Bullshit' points out it's no longer enough to have a trey deuce in your bubble goose, now you've got to pack a mac in your knapsack, and keep a vest to your chest cause wild Negroes cause stress. So when Freeman stared back at the young brotha with the Phillies Blunt shirt and matching hat, he was relieved to see John Boy in Blue appear over the ruffneck's shoulder. He couldn't help shaking his head at the irony, however, he was actually happy to see a cop.

"Oh well," he said to himself, "don't wanna be late for economics."

As he walked to class he thought back to the train, and his thoughts of the train carried him back to an earlier run in with his younger brother. Earl had come in with his pants sagging down damn near by his ankles, and Freeman told him to pull his pants up. "Yo', why you tree-ippin', money, chee-ill, get off the back black, cut a brotha some slack, chill!" Freeman, had to laugh to himself, he thought about when he was a little nappy headed boy, and brothas use to wear dangling shorts slightly exposing their nylon boxers matching their crisp nylon shirts, now the younger brothas, and nowadays joined by the younger sistas, (witness TLC), had taken it even further. "Damn," he chuckled, "black people can make a style out of anything."

Just as Freeman was ready to laugh it off, however, he heard 'Ruffneck' screaming through the speakers of his brother's headphones. "Damn, Earl! Didn't I tell you about playin' that shit? What, wha, wuss-up wit' you man, why you listenin' to that, You know that shit is wack."

"Yo', it's just a record."

"No, it's not just a record, it's propaganda. It's tellin' young brotha's that that's what they should be and young sista's that that's what a real man is, and that she's supposed to be a 'Gangsta Bitch' ('now that you saw Apache's video'). I know you know better than that, at least I hope you do, you ain't stupid! Give me that fuckin' tape."

"Yo', don't mess up my tape."

"Man, I ain't gonna destroy your tape, I wanna play it. I want you to think about her image of a positive young black man. On the down low, he's playin' cee-low, he's sportin' a mouth filled to the brim wit' gold teeth, and to top it off, startin' shit is how he gets relief! I mean, yo', what kind of madness is this?" Freeman asked. "She says she needs a ruffneck, that's swift and quick to get stiffed. Now I know you ain't smokin' no spliffs, so what's up wit' that? Pissin' in corners, not showin' any respect, are you pissin' in corners and showin' no respect?"

"No!"

"So, how you gonna patronize this?"

"You, got a point. Can I ask you this though?"

"Go ahead."

"You listen to Ice Cube, don't you?"

"Yeah." Freeman sensed that he was walking on thin ice. He remembered reading an article by Hunter College alumnus David Lamb, 'Ice Fog: Amerikkka's Most Wanted - Cubed', analyzing Ice Cube's first solo album 'Amerikkka's Most Wanted', exploring the author's own tussle with the joy he derived from listening to Ice Cube's detailed descriptions of the social pathologies rampant in ghetto life. Freeman also thought of the positive records Ice Cube had made, some of which held up a seriously needed critical mirror of the ills Black people in Amerikkka have to confront. Freeman considered Cube's 'Us' to be one of the most extraordinarily powerful records ever made.

Like Ice Cube, Freeman also wondered what had unleashed our animal instinct, why an accidental step on a brotha's sneakers could result in a 'beat-down'. Superstition, cruelty and vice seemed to be the order (or rather the disorder) of the day. And he, like Ice Cube, was just tryin' to make sense out of a senseless world.

Chapter Sixteen

"Yo', I almost had to get wit' this kid today, O.K."

"Oh yeah, wassup?"

"Well I was ridin' to school on the train this mornin', and one kid was about to vic another kid for his leather knapsack, so I asked the kid wussup, leave the dude alone."

"What?! You crazy, dude, he'd a had to handle it. Why'd you do that?"

"I know, but I was still angry from last night."

"Last night? Why?"

"Well, remember I went to have dinner at Angelita's house?"

"Oh yeah, yeah, how'd that go, boyeeee?"

"I thought it went ah-ight, but her family's bugged."

"Why you say that?"

" 'Cause her brother is married to some Russian woman he ordered through the mail, and because Angelita's mom's doesn't want her to go out wit' me 'cause I'm black." Malady who'd just finished eating lunch, came along just as Freeman was finishing, and just in time for O.K. to ask: "'Cause you black?"

"Yo', man, I told you, she's crazy."

"Well, if you ask me . . ."

"We didn't ask you, Malady." O.K. stated flatly.

"Well, if you did ask me, it serves you right. You brothas are finally getting a taste of your own medicine."

"What are you talkin' about?" An agitated Freeman asked.

"Well you know, you brothas are always after those lightskin women."

"Well, Malady, first of all I don't think that's true."

"Then explain videos, why do all the women have to look like that."

"Well first of all who's doin' the castin'," O.K. chimed in, "most of those rappers have very little control over their videos, and second of all that's not true, what about the video L.L. did for '6 Minutes of Pleasure' where it's just him and this darkskin sista wit' a short natural just kickin' it?"

"That's the exception proving the rule. What about when that brotha said: 'red-bone booties I love to smack'?"

"All right, you got me on that one, but the brotha just needs to be educated about his history anyway, after all he also said, 'Dizzy Gillespie plays the sax'."

"You gotta admit them boyz can rap though," O.K. chimed in.

"Well, what about when sistas are walking down the street and brothas are like: 'pssst, pssst, yo' lightskin?'"

"Oh, oh, and brothas never say: 'pssst, pssst, yo' darkskin, yo' chocolate,'" O.K. responded defiantly.

"Yeah, yeah they do," Malady conceded, "but it's an insult." Freeman, who'd been somewhat sympathetic to Malady's side, even though he felt that it was somewhat self-serving, divisive and dangerous, and also limited his options (or at least required that he second guess his own choice - after all, what did this say about him and Angelita? Had he too been swayed by the videos?), felt compelled to confront Malady on her last comment.

"So, Malady you're sayin' that when a brotha says "hey, darkskin" to a sista, it's an insult, but when a brotha says 'hey, lightskin,' it's a compliment?"

"That's right."

"Now, see, I can't see that. To me, as far as Ah'm concerned if you feel that way then you're the one with the problem, because in both cases the brotha is just tryin' to buss-a-move. It really doesn't matter what she looks like, he'll use whatever, if she's fat, he'll say: "I like 'em thick," if she's skinny, he'll say: "What's up, slim," so if there's a problem, it's in your own mind."

"No. No, I don't think so. Why does he have to bring up color at all?"

"Well, that's true, I agree, but I still say, that in that example the brotha wasn't expressin' no preference, he was just describin' the person."

"Now come on Freeman, now, you know brothas have preferences. You know that's why they go out with Spanish girls, they want to go out with white girls, but can't get them, so they go after what they think is the next best thing - light skin and long hair."

"See, now that's the problem, as far Ah'm concerned Latinos are part of the African Diaspora. And that sentiment reflects your own insecurities. If you know your history then you know that the slave ships didn't just stop in English speakin' countries. It was Carlos Cooks, a Dominican, who started the 'Buy Black' campaign in Harlem, and I know you know Schomburg was Puerto Rican, so what you sayin'?"

"Well, anyway, I've got to go to class." Malady said, before riding off into the sunset.

"You, know what her problem is? She's fat." O.K. decided.

"Yeah," Freeman sighed, before sucking his teeth in frustration, "I don't know though, everything's so damn complicated." He was second guessing his taste.

Chapter Seventeen

"Here Freeman, listen to my report," Angelita said, as they sat in his father's private study room. "Let me read," she said, as she began, "during preparation for the 1980 U.S. Census there was intense debate as to what to call Spanish speaking Americans, Latino, His-panic, Spanish speaking, Spanish surnamed, Spanish. Eventually, "Latino" was going to be used, but then it was decided that "Latino" looked and sounded too much like "Ladino" an archaic dialect of Spain, now only restricted to a small number of Spanish Jews. Finally, Hispanic, was chosen.

"Even though it was chosen, the term "Hispanic" makes an odd choice for a group that is linguistically defined. "Hispanic" is an English word meaning pertaining to Spain. One might think that since language plays such a major role in defining the group, that it would also decide its name--Latino. Latino and Latina have gender, which is Spanish, whereas Hispanic, having no gender, follows English rules.

"Moreover, "Hispanic" puts more emphasis on Spain and Portugal, de-emphasizing the Indian and African roots of Latinos.

"The closest word to Hispanic in Spanish is hispano which means Spanish-speaker. Professor Ana Celia Zentella, a linguistics specialist at the CUNY Graduate

Center, traced the origins of the word Hispanic to "Hispania" a Phoenician word for "land of rabbits." According to professor Zentella, Hispania was used to describe that part of Europe which includes present day Spain." As Angelita spoke, Freeman, smiled to himself, he loved the way her African-American inspired inflections complemented her Spanish accent, and he wondered, if just maybe he was having a positive influence on her after all.

"So, how do you like it, so far?"

"Yo', I think it's great."

"Really?"

"Really," he said as he leaned in with a gentle kiss.

Chapter Eighteen

As his lips floated away from hers, Angelita watched in stunned amazement as his mouth opened wide and attempted to swallow her left breast - in one fell swoop - whole! And then she saw his cheeks puff out like Dizzy Gillespie's as her breasts were massaged by his mouth; and then he drew back, as if to admire his handiwork, looking over her body: first, her womanhood, still safely hidden inside her Levi's; then, her naked navel, whereupon he licked his labios. Next? Her bare pechos, and then he looked into her ojos, She tried in vain to hide her enjoyment, but she was overwhelmed, and the eyes being the windows to the soul, gave her away. And then he began kissing her breasts anew, but not like before, this time his tongue gently stroked her nipples, and her breasts became firm, trumpeting a new level of excitement. He tried to unzip her pants, She laughed when he realized in frustration that they were 'button down'! His lips floated back to hers, as he smothered her face in kisses, hoping to

distract her as he sought to unbutton her 'button downs'.
"Why don't I stop him?!" She silently screamed to herself.

> "I'm Catholic,
> I want to be a doctor -
> I don't want to get pregnant,
> my mother would kill me,
> my grandmother would have a stroke,
> my Papi might stroke me
> I have to tell him to stop,
> I'm a virgin
> I don't want to get pregnant,
> "!Ave Maria!"
> I could hear my mother say,
> I have to tell him to stop.

"Stop," she said, so softly at first that he didn't understand her. "Freeman, please stop."

"What's wrong?" He said.

"I'm not ready for that" she said, almost embarrassed. They lay there silently for what seemed like an eternity, and every second that passed Angelita grew increasingly uncomfortable as she became ever more aware, now that the intimacy had been broken, that her breasts were exposed. Freeman reached over and played with her hair, sending shivers of excitement throughout her body. She remembered their first kiss. It was at one of their private Spanish study sessions. As she was reading an article from El Diario to him, Angelita could see that he was paying as much attention to her lips, as he was to what she was saying. She remembered, it was exactly on the word "pobre," but right at the beginning of the word, so that her lips were already puckered, he just leaned in and kissed her right on the lips. It was nice. The pizza parlor,

70th Street, Lexington Avenue - their first meeting. She was standing on line waiting to order. She felt a tap on her left shoulder. She turned. "Excuse me, are you in Prof. Lopez's Spanish class?" He asked. She knew, he knew, but went along, anyway.

Well the next thing she knew, she was studying Spanish with him in the library, and pretty soon, they had their own private study room on B2. Two weeks after that first meeting, he took her to the Center for African Art, right down the block, on 68th and Park, and later on to the Caribbean Cultural Center. She began to look forward to their 'study' sessions.

Suddenly, just as she was sinking deeper into the memories, a gentle kiss on the neck startled her back to the present. She decided that she didn't want to risk this anymore.

"Let's wait a while." She said
"Who are you, Janet Jackson?!" He said.

Chapter Nineteen

While Angelita was fending off Freeman's advances, Ralph was discovering that Olga was not so stalwart. "My love, I thank you for rescue me. It will not be longer much. I have only to be married two years, then I can become citizen even though I divorced. Ralph wants to have children, he does not know that I am taking birth control, for as you say, I do not wish to have little brown bombers.

"I miss you much, it's so hard to bear. When you were at our house for the cookout week last, i trembled when I saw you everytime. I just wantd you hold me in your arms, but I understand, as you say, we don't want Ralph to know yet, but i fear he may catch on, it is become harder for me to let him hold me, he asks why i seem so cold lately.

"Oh' Steve, when will you take me away?"

As Ralph read the letter, his heart could not believe what his eyes were reading. He felt angry, and betrayed, that the woman, whom he had rescued from the bowels of Soviet economic despair, was cheating on him! With someone he knew! His brother in blue, his friend, his buddy, Steve Violet, whom he'd welcomed into his home. Olga was right. Ralph had suspected that something was wrong. He had wondered why she no longer seemed to share his passion, but he never thought that she was cheating on him, let alone with his friend. As he ran it through his mind, he worked himself into a rage as he thought of all the times his 'brother in blue' had been by his house for cookouts. Once in his eagerness, Ralph could see now, Steve had even come by looking for a cookout when none had been planned. He had to confront him, it was Wednesday night, and he knew Steve would be at SCORES watching the Rangers game, in between beaming at the bare breasted dancing women, with the other white boys in blue. As he drove into the city, his anger increased. He'd already confronted Olga and told her that she had to go. She'd begged and cried, she had nowhere to go, she didn't know anyone in America, what would she do? "Huh, that's your problem," Ralph had said in response to Olga's pleadings. When he arrived at SCORES, Ralph was breathing heavily, by the time he left the scene he was barely breathing.

Chapter Twenty

"Curly haired nigger, shut yo' mouth if you love your family! Don't fuck with the Blue Order!" It was all so strange to Ralph, one minute he was happily married to a white Russian woman, and his mother was overjoyed, the next minute he finds out that his wife is having an affair with one of his precinct buddies, one whom he had thought he could trust with his life, let alone his wife. And then, when in an angry rage he drove to Manhattan, and confronted his blue brother, he was savagely beaten, by several indigo uniformed white boys. Now as he sat in his mother's living room reading the anonymous, cryptic letter that had been slipped under his mother's door the day after he was taken to the hospital following the beating he was feeling ashamed. Ashamed that he had accused Lloyd Finley and Eric Adams, the president and first vice president, respectively, of the Guardians, of making the Blue Order up. Ralph had condemned them, when that past December they'd prodded the FBI into launching an investigation into the source of a racist letter congratulating white officers on the shooting of Derwin Pannel, the black transit police officer, who was shot twenty-one times by white officers who mistook the undercover Pannel for a mugger, as he attempted to arrest a white woman who had illegally snuck onto the train system. The letter threatened that Lloyd Finley, Eric Adams and the Guardians would be next. The congratulatory Pannel letter, like the letter slipped under Ralph's mother's door was signed "THE BLUE ORDER." Pannel's letter also had a swastika at the bottom. At least twenty-four white officers in the transit police department's District 1 command in Manhattan received copies of the Pannel letter. Transit PBA president, Ron Reale, (who would later become a losing candidate in the Public Advocate race) questioned the existence of the Blue Order and suggested that the letter was a publicity seeking stunt. (Isn't that what they always say though? Black people are paranoid.) The Guardians, however, didn't see the letter as a prank nor as an idle threat. Adams had previously received threatening phone calls, and on a Sunday in December he'd found a dead rat on the hood of his car. He was concerned that desperate individuals would move from character assassination, as had befallen George Latimer, the city's highest ranking black transit cop, who was accused in an anonymous letter of being too drunk to attend a news conference following the shooting of Pannel, to outright physical assassination.

Now, although he was recovering from his physical wounds, Ralph had painful tears in his eyes. He was contrite and apologetic as he told the members of the department's Hispanic Society that had come to interview him of his past crimes. How at the time of the Pannel shooting, he had condemned the criticism of the department by Black and Latino officers over their disproportionate placement in dangerous undercover assignments. Assignments, they argued, that were made even more dangerous by the additional danger of being shot by white officers mistaking them for suspects, (charges that had a long history in the department). How he had strongly condemned the Guardians and the Hispanic Society, and had sided with white officers in bar room discussions concluding that the only color that mattered, was blue. And now, he had to confront the sad fact, that he had been duped, or at least had duped himself. In his mad desire for acceptance, he had rejected his Latino heritage, married a white woman, moved to Long Island, joined the National Guard, fought in the Gulf War with an irrepressible and unmatched fervor, angrily marched with the other officers in opposition to the Civilian Complaint Review Board, and he was still just "a curly haired nigger." It all hit him with the force of a tidal wave, as he wiped his face dry of teary water, and rested his head in his palms, gathering himself.

Some of those present, felt that it was good for him, that he had brought it on himself, and that he should have been a member of the Society from the beginning. In spite of these negative feelings, however, the Hispanic Society had decided to get involved, anyway, because, after all, the issue was bigger than Ralph.

It's odd how someone who never considered himself or herself a political activist, or who in fact may have been apolitical, can suddenly through the course of events become thrust into the position of being a symbol, if not a spokesperson for issues much larger than themselves. 'And when in the course of human events' such an occurrence occurs, the 'symbols' find that they have to rise to the circumstance, or face ridicule and/or scorn when they never even anticipated being in such a position before. When Rodney King was being chased by police that night, he had no idea that his life was about to change so dramatically, about to become so public. Suddenly a domestic conflict would become national news. King found himself wanted for interviews. His attendance at a baseball game would become news. And his appearance and initial lack thereof during the Los Angeles insurrection would subject him to both praise and scorn as the refrain 'Can't we all just get along' became a joke in much of black America. (See 'Posse' by Mario Van Peebles for evidence.) Now Ralph found himself becoming a symbol for issues much larger than himself, and ones that he never cared to, or at least never wanted to deal with. Before the magnitude of this turn of events had even sunk into him, the Hispanic Society was already preparing a news conference to be held outside of One Police Plaza in downtown Manhattan calling for a special prosecutor to be appointed to investigate his beating. And Freeman had already asked Angelita to speak to him about being interviewed for the Shield.

Despite his burgeoning remorse, however, Ralph took solace from the fact that throughout this entire ordeal his partner, Gary Fox, had stuck by him. It made him feel deep down, that despite the admonitions of Black and Latino officers, that cops were truly boys in the police brotherhood. That perhaps his conflict was simply personal and not racist. He and Gary spent long hours into the night discussing what happened. Gary expressed concern that the Hispanic Society was making a racial issue out of a domestic dispute. Ralph wanted to agree with him, but the chilling Blue Order letter kept splashing him with a dose of cold reality. Gary, on the other hand, simply dismissed the letter as a jerk prank. As far as Ralph was concerned, they'd always been on the up and up with each other, and after talking to Gary, Ralph was seriously considering disavowing his support of a special prosecutor for fear that he was being used as a racial battering ram. He even considered coming out for Giuliani as a symbol of racial healing and police unity.

Chapter Twenty-one

While counseling Ralph seemed a noble gesture, Freeman suspected that Gary had motivations of his own. He just didn't trust him, and on those occasions when he was present when Gary attempted to blame the Hispanic Society for making Ralph's beating a racial issue, Freeman spoke his mind, vigilantly reminding Ralph that he was just a "curly haired nigger." Needless to say, as a result of these confrontations, Freeman and Gary were not the best of buddies. As far as Freeman was concerned, Gary was just what his last name implied, a fox, and it was his duty to remind Ralph that the fox and the wolf are both after the same thing.

Hurt and confused, Ralph didn't know what to do. The Blue Order letter had forced him to confront certain realities, but he still felt that Gary was sincere - Ralph was a poor judge of character. And although Freeman's distrust of Gary in large part grew out of his general distrust of white people, his sweeping indictment on this occasion would indeed prove prescient; for Gary's motivation was indeed far from noble.

Chapter Twenty-two

"Geez, Gary don't you think we might be going too far . . ."

"No! No, Steve, I don't think we're going too far. Let me ask you a question, do you want that spic talking? You know we can't afford publicity, it might interfere with our business."

"Yeah, I know you're right, but this Gary?!"

"Come on Steve, don't get cold feet."

"I'm not getting cold feet, Gary, but Christ, can't we come up with a better cover, I mean we might not even need a cover, after the beating we gave that guy he's probably afraid to talk anyway."

"I'm just making sure he doesn't talk, Chris, just making sure. Isn't that what we all want?"

"Sure, Gary, I want the nigger to keep quiet, but this Blue Order stuff . . .? Do we even know if it really exists, and if it does they might not like us throwing their name around."

"I agree with Chris, Gary."

"Look, Steve, all I know about them is that after that spook transit officer got shot they sent around congratulatory letters. Was it a publicity stunt? I don't know, but we all know that we've got some good ol' boys in the force that make you and I look like the Kennedys!"

"Yeah, the Kennedys." They laughed.

"Look, Chris, Steve, we're coming at him from both sides, we sent him that Blue Order stuff to shake him up, but now I'll keep playing the liberal white friend. You and I know he wants to be white, that's why he married Olga in the first place-a mail order bride. I mean come on, he's just looking for an excuse to get out of it, when I get through he'll be down at One Police Plaza denouncing the spic Society."

"What's taking so long though, Gary," Steve asked, "you've been working on him a while now?"

"Look, Steve, don't complain about how long it's taking, if you hadn't been fucking his wife with such regularity, we wouldn't even have had this problem."

"You were fucking her, too, now Gary, come on."

"Yes, but I said with such regularity. And plus I stopped, but no, you, you had to make the commie think you loved her, that you were going to marry her, so you, don't you get started. Don't worry, I'll get him, there's just one little problem."

"What's that?"

"His sister's boyfriend, this little smart aleck nigger college student who thinks he's C. Vernon Mason and Al Sharpton combined."

"Should we pay him a little visit?" Chris and Steve asked. "You know we can pay him a special visit." Gary looked at Chris and Steve like a proud father, after all it was he who'd taught them how to interrogate a prisoner, how to use any materials available from a chair leg to a hanger to make a prisoner cooperative. He'd also taught them how to grab a prisoner by the throat and threaten to strangle him. This way you wouldn't leave any facial bruises, and you'd scare the hell out of him and get a confession! So Gary knew that if Freeman needed to be paid a visit, they would do it, but he also knew that the heat was on now because of Ralph's beating and because the Mollen Commission's hearings were going on. Moreover, Gary still believed that he could sway Ralph to his side. And so he granted Freeman a reprieve, temporarily.

"No, I don't think so, not yet anyway. I still think Ralph trusts me, and I can convince him that he's being used."

Chapter Twenty-three

While, Gary was expressing his concerns to his comrades in arms, Freeman was busy trying to persuade Angelita to convince her brother that Gary was not to be trusted. He had no proof, but something just didn't add up to him. He wasn't sure, but there was something phony about Ralph's Blue Order letter. Freeman remembered reading that the letter in Pannel's case had a swastika at the bottom of it, but Ralph's didn't. And he couldn't help wondering how they knew where Ralph's mother lived. The quickest way he knew to find out if Gary, as he was beginning to suspect, had some connection with the Blue Order was to drop Gary's name off with his uncle, Tom, who worked down at the Police Department's Internal Affairs Division. Since the Nixon era, Uncle Tom had maneuvered to become what he termed a 'player'. As an orderly law man he had so often defended the police against charges of racism and brutality (Eleanor Bumpurs,

Michael Stewart) that he had lost count. Being called a
'sellout' was just part of the price he had to pay to get
where he was going, he told himself. He was well aware
that he was being used, but he was a willing tool - he had
his own agenda.

Tom was pleased with himself when Al Sharpton
attacked him. If only Roy (Phil Caruso's favorite black
candidate) Innis knew how to play the game better. (Tom
had recently lost faith in Innis as a media monger;
regarding him like he did "all the others - talking loud,
saying nothing," he said. Not Tom though, when he got
where he was going he would see to it that more black
cops got recruited and moved up the ranks. Colin Powell
was his hero. He was just following the path of all those
black generals who had made the Army the most open
branch of the armed forces for blacks. Since Reagan's
election, Uncle Tom had waited patiently, plotted brilliantly
(if he did say so himself) for the day he became a player.
"Power! That's the key," he said.)

It was all coming together now, if he just played his
cards right, he would be the new top dog at I.A.D. - once
Rudy took over.

Chapter Twenty-four

"Hey uncle Tom, what's up, it's me, Freeman."
"Hey, Free, longtime no see. How are you doing,
man, I still owe you a Knicks game from last season, don't
I?"
"Yes you do."
"Yeah, I know, I was so busy, but I'll get you this
season."
"I know, the ladies, the ladies, how are they
treating you anyway?"

"Well. Very Well."

"Well, listen, unc, nuff of the light chitter chatter, I've got a serious favor to ask you."

"Anything Free, you know that."

"Well I don't know, unc, this kind of involves a police matter."

"What are you talking about, Free?"

"Well it's a long story, the bottom line is I think this cop has been harassing my girl and her family."

"Get outta here, you're serious?"

"Yeah, unc, I am serious."

"What makes you think so?"

"Let's just say I've got a hunch."

"Well you know us folk over here at Internal Affairs just love busting bad cops."

"Well, I just want you to check the grapevine and tell me what you hear."

"You got it man, what's this cats name?"

"Gary Fox."

"Is he white?"

"As cocaine."

Chapter Twenty-five

> El Negro no se lo hace a la entrada,
> lo hace en la salida.
> (If a Black doesn't mess up in the beginning,
> he'll mess it up at the end.)
>   Puerto Rican folkloric saying

While his uncle checked out Gary, and with the mayoral race swinging into high gear - with election day a month away - the Shield sponsored a meeting of representatives from the various CUNY campus organizations representing Black and Latino students to see if they could form a united front behind the Dinkins' reelection bid.

Freeman was concerned that the Latino students were going to be particularly antagonistic to Dinkins. It was clear from all of the media coverage, and from his calculated alliance with Herman Badillo that Giuliani was intent on making inroads into that voting bloc. Dinkins himself had recently been momentarily rocked by the defection of his fire commissioner Carlos Rivera to the Giuliani campaign. And by Rivera's charge that some members of the Dinkins' administration treated Hispanic officials with disdain and disrespect. (Ironically, Rivera had himself been appointed by Dinkins, and so being, became the first Puerto Rican or Latino to head a uniformed department in New York City.) Convinced that Dinkins was sure to come under attack, Freeman figured that the best defense is a good offense, so as soon as someone said that Dinkins hadn't looked out for Latinos, he laid into them with a barrage of facts he'd assembled for the occasion.

"Look, I understand that Dinkins may not be the mayor you expected him to be, or that he could be. And I know he kisses up to white folk too much sometimes, but I think you've got to compare him against his predecessors and against Giuliani, if you do that, then I think you'll be constrained to conclude that you've got to back the Mayor. Dinkins has appointed more Latinos, thirty-three, to high-level positions, than any other Mayor in history; *youknowwhatah'msayin*. As Deputy Mayor for Health and Human Services Cesar Perales is in charge of a third of the city's budget. And Gladys Carrion is the Commissioner of the Community Development Agency. Sally Hernandez-Piñero is head of the city's Housing Authority, Dennis deLeon is Chair of the Human Rights Commission, Josephine Nieves is Commissioner of the Department of Employment, and under her commissionership and Dinkins mayoralty, that department is spending over $48 million to address the high unemployment and dropout rates in Latino neighborhoods, and is implementing the Latino Training Employment Initiative, and . . ."

"Yeah, well what about Dr. Carrillo and Carlos Rivera?" Someone shouted.

"Well, I mean, if it wasn't for Dinkins, Rivera wouldn't ever have been in that position in the first place. Do you think Giuliani or Koch would've appointed a Puerto Rican fire chief?!"

"Yeah, Freeman, but it's not just about appointments, Dinkins hasn't really come through in funding community projects the way he should have."

"Yeah, Manny, I think you might have a point there. I'll tell you this, though, Dinkins has implemented a program setting a goal for the city to grant 20% of city contract dollars to firms owned by people of color and women. And since he's been in office city contracts have gone from under 9% going to people of color and women in Koch's last year to about 18% under Dinkins. And yo', don't forget Washington Heights, how do you think Giuliani would've responded? All I know, is according to Guillermo Linares, it was Dinkins' evenhanded approach to the Washington Heights conflagration that prevented an even larger explosion. Dinkins has provided Washington Heights wit' seven-day-a-week access to a school for recreation and community-service activities. And under Dinkins, the city has played a major role in renovating La Marqueta. Furthermore, under Dinkins, the City has established a community clinic in East Harlem, now you know how inadequate East Harlem's health care has been historically."

"Well, that might be true, but what about his politics. I mean in the Public Advocate's race, he should've backed Roberto Ramirez, instead he sat on the fence, which in effect meant he was backing Mark Green."

"I agree, I mean, he should've taken a stand, maybe it was because David Patterson also ran, and he felt himself in a bind, I don't know."

"Well, that's another thing, why did Patterson have to run, you know, we're tryin' to build this coalition of color in the City, and Patterson runs against Ramirez?!" (Interestingly, the day after Dinkins' victory over Roy (Phil Caruso's favorite black candidate) Innis in the Democratic primary, the New York Times reported that numerous elected officials felt that Dinkins put forth a halfhearted get out the vote effort in the primary, in order to avert pulling out black voters who may have voted for Patterson. They speculated that he might have been fearful of having two blacks heading the Democratic line, because it could further alienate white voters come November.)

"Yo', I can't speak on that, I don't know, but you have to admit that Dinkins came out strong for Nydia Velazquez against Stephen Solarz. Look, all I'm saying is what Linares said, that Dinkins has to be judged compared to what other mayors have done. Yo', it's like Willie Colon has said, under Dinkins he has seen Latinos come from havin' no say to bein' on the edge of bein' empowered."

"Yeah, but we don't want to be on the edge of empowerment, we want to be empowered. Look how few Latino judicial appointments Dinkins has made."

"Didn't he call on Governor Cuomo to appoint a Latino to fill the vacancy created by Sol Watchler's troubles?"

"Yeah, but that was only after he was criticized at a Puerto Rican Bar Association dinner when Peter Rivera raised the issue of his judicial appointments. Look Freeman, I understand where you're comin' from, I mean, Badillo is makin' a mistake runnin' wit' Giuliani, when he doesn't even agree wit' him on some fundamental issues critical to people of color. I mean, look, Dinkins set up that affirmative-action program settin' a goal for the city to award 20% of its goods and services contracts to female and minority owned companies. And I know that since Dinkins was elected in '89, female and minority owned companies have gone from gettin' 9% to 17.5% of those contracts. And I know that that's $270 million in contracts that would dry up if Giuliani came in, and that Badillo himself supports Dinkins' program. What you've got to understand, however, is that even though Badillo is playin' himself, he's actin' on a genuine emotion, and that's the feelin' of being hurt, of being jilted. It's like Blacks always want Puerto Ricans along for the ride, but the Blacks always gotta drive, while we have to wait our turn, even though we were part of the vote. We wanna drive too!"

"Well, I guess I see how it could look like that. From our angle, though, it's like we were the ones doin' all the marchin' and fightin' and dyin' that opened up the doors in the first place, and then as soon as the doors were open they wanna let everybody else in before they let us in!"

Chapter Twenty-six

Eventually, everyone came to agree that even though Dinkins, was a flawed candidate, he was still a much better choice than Giuliani. And a series of last second get out the vote drives were set for 181st St. in Washington Heights, 116th St. in East Harlem, Jamaica Boulevard in Queens and 125th Street in Harlem, as well as election day get out the vote efforts in East Harlem and Harlem. As soon as everyone was gone, Sherry summed up her feelings. "Freeman," she said, "I told you those Latinos can't be trusted, everything's "me too," as soon as Blacks get something, then they want their share too. I mean, for example, look at the State Comptroller race, those Puerto Rican state legislators weren't even thinkin' about it, but as soon as Carl McCall's name came up, all of sudden they were pressin' for Ferrer to be appointed."

"What do you think Denroy?" Freeman asked his senior editor.

"I think we just heard that Dinkins has got a personal problem."

"And might I ask what that is?" A curious Freeman asked.

"See, this is Dinkins' problem he's got no fuckin' backbone."

"Okay, okay, what do you mean?"

"He doesn't understand that politics is about power - reward your friends, punish your enemies. Black and Latino folk put his ass in office and that's who the fuck he should be lookin' out for. Now I know, Ah'm a be called a reverse racist, but shit, he didn't win the white vote, he's not goin' to win the white vote and he needs to start actin' like that, that's politics. He won't take a damn stand. He's so afraid of offendin' white people that he can't take a damn stand. I mean damn, look at the schools' chancellor race, at first he said that all things bein' equal a Latino chancellor might be better for the City, then when he's accused of tryin' to get the Hispanic vote, the next thing you know he's writin' a letter to the Board of Education on behalf of that Italian guy from Connecticut, Tirozzi, sayin' that "race and ethnicity must not be a factor," in selectin' the schools' chancellor. I mean shit, can this guy make up his mind? It's a factor in selectin' the schools' students, shit. White parents all over are optin' out of the system, goin' to private school, Catholic school, movin' to the suburbs. I mean it seems like he be grovelin' for the white vote so hard sometimes that he just never, never seems to stand up. I mean look at Crown Heights, how you gonna compare the Yankel Rosenbaum case to the Rodney King case is beyond me. . . ."

"Why you say that?"

"Because! Because, in the first place in the Rodney King case we're talkin' about government agents, police officers who were hired to protect and serve the public (although according to Ice Cube they're actually hired to "serve, protect and break a nigga's neck") violatin' the public trust. And in the second case, we're talkin' about the sanctionin' of criminal conduct on the part of police officers. In the King case there was no question as to whom the defendants were, they weren't allegin' any mistaken identity they were arguin' that their actions did not constitute a crime. In the Rosenbaum case, first of all, the defendant was a civilian not a state actor, and in the second case, the brotha wasn't arguin' that there was no crime committed he was sayin' that it wasn't him, so when the jury acquitted him they weren't sanctionin' Rosenbaum's murder, they were sayin' the police blew the investigation. When the jury acquitted the four officers in the King case, however, they were sanctionin' the actions of the police and sayin' that it's all right to beat a nigger's ass!"

Chapter Twenty-seven

'To beat a nigger's ass,' wasn't all right in Freeman's eyes, however, and the appalling outcome of the first Rodney King beating trial had helped push him to go to law school; every now and again he'd check in on his professors to make sure that his letters of recommendation were getting done. This day he went to see professor Elizabeth Al, his former political science professor whom he had singularly impressed as a freshman by shining brilliantly in her class, and who had taken him under her wing since then. She'd encouraged Freeman's plans to graduate in three years, and had pulled some strings to get him admitted into the CLIO program after what normally would have been his sophomore year, even though it was supposed to be for students who were between their junior and senior years. She had argued successfully that since he was going to be graduating in three years he was for all intents and purposes a junior, and that if they didn't allow him to participate then, they would be effectively barring his participation forever. The nickname Libby was bestowed upon her by her fellow professors who thought that the way Libby ran together with Al, accurately described her interest in 'minority' students, and she became known as 'the Libby-Al Professor', a title she seemed to relish in and tried to live up to by becoming an expert on a wide variety of programs specifically geared toward minority students interested in going to graduate school or to law school.

"So. Freeman, how do you think you'll do on the LSAT, well, I hope."

"I expect to do well, Professor Al."

"Libby!"

"Libby."

"Well, so, how do you think you'll do?" She asked again.

"Let's just say I'll be walking the halls of NYU next year."

"I always did like your modesty, Freeman," she kidded him, before causing the conversation to take a sudden turn left when she, as liberal whites are apt to do sometimes, relayed a *subtlely obvious*, probing anecdote from her own life. Even after having witnessed this phenomenon on so many occasions that he'd lost count, Freeman was still unable to tell if these anecdotes were intended to evidence the speaker's liberalism or to probe and pry a response out of the black listener, so that by so doing the speaker would then feel that they knew where all black people stood on the issue. And in some cases affirm or modify their position to what they perceived to be the politically correct one, at least as far as they could tell, not being black and all.

In any event, on this particular occasion, Professor Al was excited about the upcoming mayoral election and was agitated that her own party -- she was a member in good standing of New York State's Liberal Party -- had once again, she felt, deserted their sensibilities by backing the Republican Rudolph Giuliani. She spoke with a simmering fury, because she was convinced, especially after her recent run in with another professor, also a member of the Liberal Party, that the Party's support of Giuliani was laced with a strain of racism. Moments before Freeman had come to see her, Professor Al had had an intense debate with her colleague over his fervent support of Giuliani. She'd learned from grueling questioning that his support of Giuliani was based primarily on one issue - crime. She pointed out that according to recently released FBI statistics, crime in the City had gone down under Dinkins. Her friend responded that, while that may have been generally true, the number of murders had gone up, and that Giuliani supported the death penalty, which both he and Giuliani believed to be a deterrent to violent crime. Professor Al, was exasperated at this point because she knew, and knew that her friend should know that, the imposition of the death penalty is a matter of state law, that it's not the mayor's responsibility (though her friend responded that the mayor could help bring political pressure to bear on Albany). She retorted that Dinkins had legitimate accomplishments in the area of crime, including his initiating the padlocking of neighborhood nuisance buildings, particularly crack houses, the addition of 6,000 police officers, including 3,500 patrolmen. Her colleague remained unimpressed, (and unimpressable), and concluded that Dinkins simply did not have the proper temperament to be mayor. Dinkins he felt was too careless with the public purse, when it came to using it for self-aggrandizement. Apparently the professor's sensibilities had been permanently bruised by Dinkins purchase of a federal style headboard, built by a city carpenter, for $11,074. Yet this same professor had scarcely raised a peep over the $53,000 barbecue kitchen former mayor Ed Koch had built for City Hall or the $71,000 the former Mayor spent for an attic apartment for his indispensable gourmet chef - after all, he had to have him available, never know when an emergency gourmet meal would be needed; nor did he raise a clamor when the illustrious former Mayor spent $6,625 on oak laptop dinner trays. Professor Al smelled a double standard.

Chapter Twenty-eight

"Yo', Yo', wussup, Ice Cube's in the hi-ouse! We in there tonight, money."

"What you talkin' about, O.K.?" Freeman, asked.

"I just heard on BLS that Ice Cube is goin' to be at the Palladium tonight!"

"Stop, lyin'."

"Yo', Ah'm not lyin'. Denroy already said he's down. We in there, are you?"

"Yo', I got a practice LSAT exam on Saturday I need to study for."

"Dude! Ice Cube at the Palladium, I know you ain't frontin' on that."

"Come on now, you know me, Ice Cube, you know ah'm in there."

Going into the Palladium that night, the first thing Freeman noticed was the heavy security in effect. First off, they had to walk through a metal detector, he assumed that it worked. After going through the metal detector, they then had to go through a pat down search, and the security guard even asked Freeman to take off his shoes and shake them out. "Damn," Freeman said, "that's a change." Funkmaster Flex, from Hot 97 was rocking the wheels of steel, and composed some of the funkiest mixes Freeman had ever heard. When he heard Super Cat's 'Don Dada', playing with the bassline from Big Daddy Kane's 'Aint No Half-Steppin', the funkiest bassline in history, as its subtext, he was in Hip Hop Heaven! Doug E. Fresh showed up to rock the mic' for a minute. For some reason,

Freeman was particularly disturbed when Doug E. asked "all the real muthafuckas" to put their hands in the air. It saddened him to hear Doug E. curse. It didn't even sound right. For some reason it reminded him of Al Sharpton's justification for getting his hair fried, that it was in honor of his hero and friend James Brown, but it seemed to Freeman, that if you're going to be a leader, then you have to lead. And if that means being the example then so be it, something about Sharpton's answer was like the blind leading the blind. And Freeman actually liked the work Sharpton had done in the Senate race. But, following J.B.'s straightened hair bit, was like Doug E. following the association of Blackness with vulgarity. At the same time, however, Freeman loved Ice Cube. There was something cathartic in hearing a brotha talk shit, and get paid for it, and say what you want to say to white folk at work or in school every day, when they do something stupid or racist to piss you off.

Freeman, O.K. and Denroy had a ball laughing at the white hip hoppers, some things were just funny to them; even when they got the dances, white hip hoppers, still lack the critical discerning ear. No matter what record comes on they do the same dance. Freeman and the boys were nearly rolling on the floor as two whitegirls who must've just come from practicing moves they'd seen on Yo' MTV Raps, came running on to the floor and launched into their latest steps, without care for what was playing. This of course was not universally true, some of them had some rhythm going. (Nonetheless, however, white people still have to rely on the reaction of Black people to decide if a record is good or not. Watch the dance floor in a club, when the record changes if it's good there's usually a crowd reaction, ofttimes, a whiteboy jumps out there before Black people have assessed the quality of the record, and foolishly plays himself by giving an excited reaction, as Black people grumble and give it the thumbs down, and then the sad sack has to try and subtlely withdraw his initial reaction and join the disgruntled masses. If you're not inclined to go to a club, then go to a chain store record shop, pick any one, watch as Black people come in and the store clerks ask them if they need any help, the brothas and sistas usually react by saying, "that's all right, I got it covered." On the other hand, watch white folk, when they come in they can't wait for a clerk to come over and direct them as to what records are good or not, as to what they should buy. Black folk are the musical tastesetters of America, and have been since they got off the boat.)

As the Japanese hip-hop tourist crowded onto the dance floor, O.K. suddenly found himself standing next to this Japanese cutie. Now, O.K. was not the kind of brotha to front, so he turned around and obliged the young lady. As his mouth approached her ear to ask her for her number, O.K. was distracted by the bumrush of the crowd toward the stage as the curtain rose, and Ice Cube's name flashed across the stage. The crowd was sadly disappointed, however, when Mad Flava rolled out, Freeman, O.K. and Denroy were among the most disappointed; they just couldn't get into the idea of whiteboys trying to rap, period. As O.K. turned away from the stage to resume his conquest, he found the source of his interest gone. "Damn!" He cried, "you've got to take advantage of the moment." While they couldn't get into Mad Flava, they had to give props to their dee jay, an Asian looking kid who had mastered the art of cutting and scratching.

"Yo', that Chinese kid was dope!" Denroy exclaimed.

"Indeed he was," Freeman concurred.

"Ah, he was ah-ight," O.K. said unenthusiastically, revealing a little competitive jealousy. As they waited for Ice Cube to come on, all three scoped the crowd like hawks lookin' over a field of chickens. Freeman's hunt was interrupted when he suddenly found himself enveloped by a gust of indo smoke. "Damn," he coughed, "what the fuck was that?! There's more cheeba in here than a school yard. . . ."

The menacin' sound of the theme from Jaws signaled Ice Cube's approach to the stage, and the crowd brimmed with eager anticipation, for their anti-hero hero to deliver the goods. And he didn't disappoint - even though the sound system was wack. The most memorable part of the show, however, turned out not to be Cube's performance, but the interruption thereof by King Sun, who Ice Cube said accused him of stealin' his hit record, 'Wicked' from him. As King Sun issued a challenge over the speaker, that he would see Ice Cube later, Cube responded defiantly": "Fuck, later, see me now!" And then put down his mic, apparently ready to rumble, as the brothas next to the trio, roared their approval. "Yo', that Ice Cube ain't no joke." "I told you that muthafucka is real." "Yo' King Sun, 'bout to get done." "Yo', fuck dat, dis is New York, he betta take dat shit back to L.A." "Man you crazy, Ice Cube is runnin' shit in nine d 3." And so on, and so on it went.

After the show, as they rode the iron horse home, Freeman and crew assessed the evening. "Yo', when King Sun came over the mike, I thought it was just part of the show," Denroy said.

And it seemed like a set up for 'Check Yo' Self', O.K. chimed in, "but, then when Ice Cube was performin' he seemed upset, for real, and shit. And then when he stepped off without even performin', 'It Was A Good Day', I was like damn! I was waitin' for him to rock that."

"But, yo', the most fuck'd up thing is that when I go home, Ah'm gonna have to put all of my clothes in the cleaners 'cause Ah'm smellin' like indo from head to toe," Freeman griped.

"Yeah, that shit was wack, I was hopin' the dee jay would put on KRS' new joint, 'I Can't Wake Up', you know the one where Kris imagines that he's a joint gettin' lit up, split up, and smoked up by a whole bunch of different rappers who be rappin' about the beauty of blunts," O.K. said.

"Yo', Ah'm glad somebody's tryin' to check that, that shit is fuck'd up. Hey yo', doesn't it seem like cheeba smokin' had calmed down a little, and now it seems like that shit is startin' to burn out of control. You know, these white controlled record companies know what they're doin'. I mean, damn, there's so many records where there's a reference to gettin' high, now, that I've lost count." Denroy added.

"Yo', but Freeman, man, I got a bone to pick wit' you my brotha."

"What are you talkin' about Denroy?"

"I heard through the grapevine that you hooked my man O.K. here up wit' Nilsa. Wussup wit' that?" Denroy asked his voice rising in a sing song fashion.

"Yo', I didn't know you were interested, and besides, I didn't hook him up, he just came to the party wit' us, he had to hook his own self up."

"So you went wit' Angelita, right?"

"Right."

"So does that mean Sherry is free, my brotha?"

"Oh snap, see how you gonna try and play me like dat?"

"Ah'm just askin'. So do she and Angelita know about each other?"

"Come on, now, chill." Just before Freeman met Angelita, he and Sherry had entered that post-relationship pre-breakup phase; where you're no longer "seeing" the person, but you still see the person all the time, and from time to time, you feel and act as though you're still "seeing" them. When Freeman first met Sherry he was captivated by her beautiful, smooth, chocolate skin, by her hair crowned in corn-rows, and by her rhythmic style of speaking, marked by its air of nobility, and its soothing grace. Over time, however, Freeman came to feel that what he had taken for nobility was in fact pretentiousness. At first he had found Sherry's pretensions somewhat humorous, they had a charm of their own, eventually though, her pretentiousness had become grating; particularly when she tried to shape him into the kind of Ebony Man buppie, he despised but she wanted him to be. He lacked her passion for dramatic flair, flamboyant capes and stunning hats. And he had a hard time reconciling her love affair with Liz Clairborne fashion with her pseudo-Afrocentricity. In his own mind, he was a new creature - the b-boy intellectual and he felt harassed and harangued by her continual efforts to get him to speak properly, to stop dropping his g's to stop wearing his baseball caps, to get a new hairstyle, something more 'buppie'. If she just left him alone he thought, she'd be all right.

"So, yo' did ya'll have fun at the party though?" Denroy asked.

"Crazy fun," O.K. chimed in, I mean it was snaps because when you see people dancin' to Salsa music the shit looks like their dancin' fast, but both Freeman and I got dogged for dancin' too fast."

"For dancin' too fast?" A confused Denroy asked.

"I know the shit sounds bugged, but it's true." Freeman explained. "See, we be listenin' to all the superstructure when we hear Salsa, all the horns and shit, that's above the base, but they be listenin' and dancin' to the base underneath, keepin' pace wit' that."

"I don't know, I'd have to see that." A disbelieving Denroy responded.

"I'm tellin' you," Freeman said, "that's the way it is. Oh yeah, O.K. did I tell you what happened to me that night?"

"Nah wussup?"

"Yo', peep this, right, me and Angelita were waitin' for a cab, it was rainin' that night right. And you and Nilsa had already stepped, so we were just waitin'. Finally one stops and we get in, and the guy, I think he was an Arab guy, is like he's not movin' unless I pay him in advance. He said that he had driven black guys before and they jump out without payin'. So I had to pay in advance. Now you know some brothas will do that shit, but you know ah'm here wit' my girl, and I don't like being accused of being no criminal, and shit, *youknowwhatah'msayin'*. So I told him, "I'm not payin' you in advance, get the fuck outta here," right. And he says, "well I'm not going." And I say, "I'm not goin' anywhere either." Then Angelita doesn't want any trouble so she says, you know, "come on let's catch another cab, this guy is just stupid," that kind of stuff, but ah'm like ah'm not gettin' out! I told Angelita not to get out! Of course she gets out anyway. And I say to the guy, something like, "you fuckin' bastard, you're lucky Ah'm wit' my girl, or else I'd fuck you up!" Now I knew this outburst would only reinforce his negative conceptions, but it's the kind of crazy thing racism makes you do sometimes. There's a kind of perverse power in havin' people fear you. It almost feels strange when a white woman doesn't clutch her purse when you go by, even though you know you're not the criminal, and that white people have some nerve after stealin' the Indian's land and kidnappin' us from our homes. Anyway, as we climbed into the back of the next cab, I saw that the driver, was East Indian, and I was just waitin' to lay into him. When it dawned on me that the guy was listenin' to Naughty-by-Nature. As the guy is drivin' he's boppin' his head to the music, not quite on beat, but not as off as white people were before black videos, just then Naughty-by-Nature goes off and Fat Joe comes on, the guy turns the radio up, and turns around and says something, but I couldn't make out what he was sayin', so he turns the radio down, and turns around, while he's drivin', and says 'I love that Fat Joe, he's great.' Angelita and I were rollin'. New York is a funny place sometimes."

Chapter Twenty-nine

As Freeman sat at his desk working on sample LSAT questions, while bobbing his head to Digable Planets, the only Hip Hop album he was really able to study to, his concentration was broken by the ring of the phone and the message of the caller.

"Freeman."

"What up?"

"This is Tom."

"Hey, unc, what's up?"

"You are."

"What you mean?"

"Seems that Fox friend of yours has been under investigation by I.A.D. for some time now."

"Really? For what?"

"I can't say, it's classified?"

"Come on, man, I'm family."

"Well, I can't talk about it here. What are you doing tonight?"

"Seeing you."

"You always were a smart kid."

"You still remember where I live, don't you?"

"Of course."

"Okay come over to my house about 8:30, I'll buy you dinner."

"Cool."

"Oh, yeah, and Freeman . . ."

"Yes."

"Say hello to your father for me."

"You got it, man." As Tom hung up, his mind flashed back to an earlier time, when his younger brother had first learned that Tom was joining the Police Academy. He remembered his brother's opening salvo: "You can't serve two masters." "Wasn't that the perennial argument?" Tom asked himself. 'That you can't be a cop and for black people at the same time.' "We have to work within the system," had been and continued to be Tom's response. He argued that if there were going to be police anyway, that it was better that he, somebody from the community serve, rather than turn the job over by default, to outsiders. His brother wasn't buying it, however, and called him a 'Buffalo Soldier', just keeping watch of the natives. "We've got to make Harlem safe. Tom had argued. "Yeah? For what Tom? For these liquor stores? For these department stores, owned by people who not only don't live here, but who don't give a fuck about the people who do!" Tom admired his brother's spirit, even though he didn't agree with him. "What about pop's store?" Tom had asked without waiting for an answer. "Did you forget about that?!" He continued. "You want to romanticize those rioters, but look what they did to pop's business. They've never built a damn thing in their lives, all they know how to do is tear down and destroy. Just crabs in a barrel, that's all, crabs in a barrel."

"You got that right. The ghetto is a barrel, a damp cramped pit, encircled and enclosed on all sides, and the only way out is to climb over one another. You put people in a barrel, and they're going to act like crabs, what else do you expect?"

"Look, I know plenty of people out here who aren't crabs, and who are sick and tired of getting pinched, robbed, intimidated and murdered by these fools. That's who I'm looking out for, the good people."

In those early days, Tom had an almost idealistic view of police service, but, alas, shit happens, things change.

Chapter Thirty

"Now, Free, you've got to promise me you won't say anything."

"Come on, unc."

"Freeman, I'm serious."

"Okay, okay, I promise."

"Okay. From what I could gather, your friend Gary, and some other cops from his precinct are under investigation for possible criminal activity. As far as I could tell from the records I saw, they're suspected of staging phony raids on crack houses all around Washington Heights, using the phony raids to cover their real aim which is to steal money, drugs and guns. Mostly, it seems they're just after cash, but sometimes those bastards take the damn cocaine and sell it back to another dealer. These cops are supposed to be protecting the community, instead they let these deals go down, so they can make a heist! And then they turn around and give this poison to some other lowlife to start the cycle all over again. And you know all of these cops are white, Long Islanders, don't even live in the damn City."

"Do, you remember if one of the cops was named Violet?"

"Why?"

"I just wanna know."

"Uh'm, yeah, yeah, one of them was named Violet."

"I knew it!" Freeman exclaimed. "I knew Gary was connected to this guy somehow."

"I don't understand, Free, who's Violet?"

"He's the one who was sticking my girlfriend's brother's wife. And all this time Gary has been acting like he's down wit' her brother, like they're boys, you-know-what-ah'm-sayin'. So what's up, unc, what are you gonna do about Gary and his crew?"

"Well I.A.D. has been frozen out of the investigation. The Division did such a terrible job investigating Michael Dowd, that Dinkins had to appoint the Mollen Commission to investigate police corruption. And from what I heard the feds have taken over this investigation. I.A.D. has just been trying to help gather evidence, but so far we haven't been too successful."

"Yeah, I read about that Dowd dude in the papers, wuss-up-wit'-that, how was he able to get away with all that for so long?"

"Well, first of all, if you read those articles carefully, you'd see that most of his dirt was done in colored neighborhoods and harmed colored folk. Right then and there, it's less important to a lot of people. Then, secondly, cops don't like turning in other cops, forget race for a second, this is just a cop thing, you know it's us against the world. You've got criminals you're scared of, but that you have to confront. Then on top of that you've got a second guessing public who wants you to protect them, but then turn against you when they think you've gotten too tough on a criminal, as if they'd know what it takes to stop a criminal. And then, thirdly, the higher ups are afraid of bad press, you know, they've got ambitions and it would be bad if all of this had been going on under their noses, so they'd rather just sweep it under the rug."

"So, what are we goin' to do?"

"I'm not sure, I've got an idea though, let me think it through."

"Yo', unc."

"Yeah?"

"Yo', unc, I think I can help."

"What are you talking about?"

"Yo', I think I can help. See, my girl, her brother and Gary are friends, at least they're supposed to be friends, though I suspect her brother is going to be shocked when he finds out about his 'friend'. Well anyway, her brother, Ralph, who is a cop, can get close to this guy, plant a bug in his apartment, or something."

"Wait a minute, I don't understand, Violet was having sex with his wife? And now you're telling me they're friends? Is your girlfriend white?"

"Oh snap, how you gonna dis me like that? Now you know I ain't meltin' no snowflakes. She's Dominican, and her brother and Gary used to be partners."

"Used to be partners, what happened?"

"Well, you probably saw in the paper that the Hispanic Society had a protest down at One Police Plaza, because a Latino officer got beat down by some off-duty white officers. Well that's her brother."

"Hmmm. I see, what's her brother's name?"

"Rafael, Rafael de Cimarrones, but he likes to be called Ralph."

"You think he'd be willing to help?"

"After all he's been through, yes, I think so."

"O.K., talk to him."

Chapter Thirty-one

As Freeman left his uncle, he was wondering how he was going to tell Ralph, after all, Ralph was already reeling and Freeman was concerned that he might do something rash and stupid like run out and confront Gary, and blow the whole game plan. He decided that he shouldn't tell Ralph over the phone, because he might hang up. "Nope, I'd better tell him in person," he said to himself.

Chapter Thirty-two

As Freeman expected, Ralph was devastated. His last hope for acceptance into white America had withered away into nothingness, and worst of all he felt like a chump, a sucker, a Blow Pop, a tootsie roll, suddenly it dawned on him that Gary had been laughing in his face the whole time, and he'd just been too blind to see it. But, now Ralph had no more tears, he was all cried out, if Gary wanted to play, then they would play, he was a cop after all, he knew the game - it was payback time. At least it would be when Freeman and Ralph figured out how to get around their next obstacle.

Chapter Thirty-three

In less than a week, Freeman's uncle's stock had dramatically risen in his nephew's eyes, He was no longer Tom, the "Tom," he was simply uncle Tom. Unfortunately, however, what goes up, must come down, and Tom's image in Freeman's mind was due to plummet.

"So what are you sayin', uncle Tom, that you're just gonna pull out like that, that you're goin' to turn and walk away. I can't believe this, we got these cops runnin' around here like they're starrin' in 'Menace II Society', and you're not goin' to do anything about it, what's goin' on?"

"You don't understand, Freeman."

"You're right! I don't understand! I'll never understand!"

"I've gotta go now Freeman, I'll call you later."

"Yeah, right," Freeman said bitterly. He was in shock. He couldn't believe his uncle, could be this much of a sucka - he was starting to feel the way his father once did about his brotha. What was he going to tell Ralph, who had already agreed to spy on Gary, and now this. He knew Ralph would feel betrayed once again. Freeman couldn't believe his uncle. He just couldn't understand.

In truth, Freeman, didn't understand. He didn't know that his uncle had been told, actually threatened, to stay off the case. That when he asked his superiors about Gary, he had been met with inferences suggesting his own involvement in the drug trade. They wanted to know how a guy on his salary could afford a condo on the East Side. Tom, knew he was clean, he knew that he had watched his money over the years, made shrewd investments. He didn't have any kids, and he was single. He also knew, however, that even if proven innocent, the mere allegation of corruption would create a stench that would follow him, as a black cop, until he was drummed off the force and publicly humiliated. No, he couldn't risk it, he thought.

Uncle Tom wanted to help but he didn't want to cross his higher ups; after all he had spent years cultivating his image as a team player, and now he was poised to leap frog up the ranks. As one of the few black cops actively supporting and working on behalf of the Guiliani campaign, Tom was expecting to reap huge benefits after a Guiliani victory. As far as he was concerned, he had come too far, and worked too hard to blow it now.

Chapter Thirty-four

"Ralph, I don't know how to tell you this," Freeman said carefully, "and I don't know why, but my uncle says that he can't go through wit' the investigation."

To Freeman's surprise, Ralph was fairly nonperturbed by his news. The latest revelation of Gary's chicanery had in some strange way rejuvenated Ralph, given him a new lease on life, and he was ready to go ahead, come what may.

"Don't worry about it, Freeman, I figured that might happen, those bastards in the Department just wanna keep everything covered up. You don't know what kind of pressure they can bring, they probably put the squeeze on your uncle. I'll tell you this, though, Freeman, I've gone as low as I can go, I can't go any lower, and the only way for me to get back on my feet is to take Gary down. So with or without I.A.D., Gary is going down."

Chapter Thirty-five

Freeman's disaffection cut Tom to the quick, childless himself, Tom saw himself as sort of a surrogate father to Freeman, he wanted to mold him in his image - a young Republican. Now Tom could hear in Freeman's voice resentment reminiscent of Freeman's father. Through all his years of toil in the force, Tom had developed the leathery thick skin many black officers feel they have to have in order to deal with the almost visceral reaction many black folk have toward the police. Black folk's perceptions didn't bother Tom, not anymore they didn't. He was a law and order man, an orderly law man. As far as he was concerned complaints about the police were simply stories told by lazy, good-for-nothing no accounts. Tom was above that. Besides he was too busy. Things were hectic down at I.A.D., the Mollen Commission's open hearings had just lit a fire under the division, as Police Commissioner Raymond Kelly found himself coming out in support of some type of independent investigative agency to examine police corruption, and the head of the division found himself transferred after being criticized at the Commission's hearings; Tom wasn't sure which way the political winds were blowing. He had a sinking feeling. Day after day the hearings and the papers exposed new levels of police corruption, ranging from pension fraud, to robbery to good 'ol fashioned police brutality, as well as exposing I.A.D.'s incompetence, inability or unwillingness to police the police. Meanwhile, Phil Caruso and the Patrolmen's Benevolent Association were running a blistering series of full page scathing attacks on Dinkins. And as the Mollen Commission brought out more and more dirt from underneath the white rug lying next to the Blue Wall of Silence, it was becoming increasingly apparent to Tom that the Commission was edging closer and closer to advising the Mayor to set up an independent watchdog agency, because the police were apparently incapable of policing themselves. His future was suddenly cloudy, he didn't know which way the winds were blowing. He had a sinking feeling. Cops all over the city were p.o.'d. Corrupt cops were reacting to the pain of the truth stepping on their toes, while honest cops felt as if all cops were being painted with the broad brush of corruption. Meanwhile, the Hispanic Society, supported by the Guardians, asked for both the Mayor's and Giuliani's support for the appointment of a special prosecutor to investigate Ralph's beating. Under the confluence of these converging events a desperate Gary felt the walls closing in on him, as he frantically searched his intoxicated mind for a way out.

Chapter Thirty-six

"Kill the mayor! Huh, I don't know about that one Gary."

"Look, you guys, I've got a cousin on the force down in Philadelphia and he told me a few years back how they were going to take care of that nigger mayor down there. Remember that whole thing with those crazy niggers, MOVE, when that nigger neighborhood got burned down, before they had a chance to do it themselves. Well some of the officers had put a plan in effect to take Mayor Goode out if he showed his spook face. (In his autobiographical memoirs, 'In Goode Faith' former Philadelphia mayor W. Wilson Goode wrote that on the eve of the fateful Move blaze "[t]hree people who had always provided [him] with useful information . . . had obtained information alleging that if [he] went to the MOVE scene, [he] would catch a bullet with his name on it!" That members of Philadelphia's Finest were going to take him out, and make it look like an accident.) We could do the same thing here, create a riot situation, it's election time, Dinkins has to come. And boom! Out of nowhere a shot is fired from somebody in the crowd, down goes Stinkins."

"But, Gary . . ."

"But, Gary," nothing. We've got all this heat coming down on us. First you idiots beat up that curly haired nigger, and now the Hispanic Society is pressing Dinkins to investigate. The damn Mollen Commission he appointed is snooping around everywhere. Look I'm telling you we get rid of Dinkins and all of this goes away. With Rudy in office, do you think he's going to give a fuck about the Hispanic Society, the Mollen Commission? Nah, Rudy loves the police."

Gary and his partners in crime had always made it a point to talk business in his police car, it was the last place in the world they'd figured anyone would bug. And it was, at least until Ralph got involved and talked Gary into taking him on a drive. Now as he listened to Gary plot Ralph couldn't believe his ears. He thought he and Gary were friends. After all, hadn't Gary stuck by him in his time of need, but what was this, he's hanging out with Steve Violet, after he slept with Ralph's wife, and now their planning to murder Mayor Dinkins. "I can't believe this."

"Quiet," Freeman said, "I'm tryin' to hear what they're talkin' about, this shit is crazy. Yo', yo' check this out, listen to this."

"So, Gary, what's up with that deal with those Rodriguez brothers?"

"The meeting is still on. I set it up for Club 2000. I want there to be a crowd around, when I'm dealing with

these crazies. And we know there won't be any police there
to spot us."

"Oh, shit, I've got to tell my uncle about this." Just
then a call came over the police radio reporting a domestic
dispute. Instead of responding to the call, however, Gary
and his cronies just laughed, there wasn't any way they
were going to the scene - why should they, they thought -
there wasn't any money to be made in a domestic dispute.
They were waiting for a drug bust or the aftermath of a
street corner pharmacist shootout, where they could clean
the victim's pockets of his ill-gotten gains. As far as they
were concerned robbing dealers was just their way of
enforcing a tax on the underground economy that eluded
the grasp of Uncle Sam.

"Are they kidding?" Chris whined. "Some guy
beating up his old lady, you know how those spic chicks
are, they like that. Now, Gary, how much you figure we
make from this deal next Saturday."

"Let me put it this way, after this weekend, that
summer house will be mine; and I can keep the wife and
kids out of the way in the summer and free myself up to
get some real pussy. Look, just stick with me, and I'll
show you how to make some real money. You see this
badge, it's a fucking license to steal. A fucking license to
steal. I'm telling you guys there are so many angles. Listen
to this, I've got this deal with this lawyer, this Australian
guy (Alligator Angelo) who has a little hole in the wall
office downtown near the criminal court, he speaks
Spanish, and whenever I grab one of these chicos from up
here me and him have got a great deal going. See, I'll get
to the court early and spot the perp's family, then I'll call
this lawyer guy up, and tell him to come right over, and
I'll tell the family about this guy being a great lawyer, if
they hire him, I get a piece of the action. For an extra-fee,

I'll fuck the affidavit up so bad that the judge will be forced to throw the case out. Now, is that funny or what?"

"Chris, did I ever tell you how me and Gary met?" Steve asked, anxious to add to the festive atmosphere. "I was fucking working in Bedford-Stuyvesant, fresh out of the Academy and straight from Long Island. I'd never been around so many niggers in my life. I was expecting Shaka Zulu to jump out from behind some tree and attack me, I'm telling you I'm jumping at my own shadow. I'm coming out of the coffee shop, and I hear this woman scream from around the corner, just as I'm turning the corner. Well this teenage jungle bunny had snatched some old woman's pocketbook, and as soon as he sees me he starts hauling ass in the other direction, the dumb prick runs right in front of the stationhouse. Gary's standing in front, not even looking and he hears me chasing the guy and starts to turn and look, and boom! The guy runs into him and they both crash to the floor, I run up with my gun drawn yelling at the fucker not to move. Gary sees this nervous rookie waving his gun and tells me to calm down, and cuffs the guy. And you know what? He takes the collar! I chase the guy down, and he takes the collar, that's when I learned about seniority."

"Those were good days," Gary said longingly, "the days before all this Mollen Commission bullshit. These fucking lawyer types are so full of shit, everybody wants to close the crack houses, but nobody wants to put the crack dealer outta business, fucking Dinkins pays for that guy's funeral. You see what just happened, those cocksuckers dropped a bucket of cement on that cop's head, just because he was trying to do his job. The only way to put them outta business is to take the profit out, you see how these dealers live better than you and I, fucking hardworking honest Americans, since the government won't tax 'em, we'll tax 'em, that's what we are, fucking tax collectors."

Chapter Thirty-seven

"Uncle Tom! Uncle Tom! . . ."

"Freeman, what's wrong, what are you so excited about?"

"I can't tell you over the phone, I've got to see you in person, unc, tonight, I've got to see you tonight."

"It's two o'clock in the morning, Free, you sure it can't wait?"

"It can't wait."

"I'm sorry Freeman it'll have to wait." As Freeman put down the phone, Rafael (as Ralph now asked to be called) was harassing him for details, was his uncle going to see them or what?

"He said it'll have to wait, and hung up." A shocked and depressed Freeman said.

Chapter Thirty-eight

Tom was in a quandary, he wanted to help Freeman, but he could not see how to make it work for him. Then suddenly, it came to him, the answer was right there on his coffee table; or rather in the paper on his coffee table. He had to laugh at the irony of it all, for it was in the Mollen Commission's very criticisms of I.A.D.'s incompetence that Tom saw his opportunity to simultaneously regain his nephew's confidence and respect and also to ingratiate himself further with the Guiliani campaign. Tom figured that through his contacts in Rudy's

campaign he could convince Guiliani that he could hand
him a high profile anti-corruption case, with the added
enticement that it would have a black and a latino cop
busting crooked white cops, thereby helping to alleviate
colored folks fear of Rudy. It was a win-win situation all
around. Tom loved it, he knew that with Guiliani backing
him his higher ups would not dare move against him. He
called Freeman the next morning and set up a meeting with
Freeman and Ralph for that evening.

Chapter Thirty-nine

"Wow! Kill the Mayor!" A frustrated Tom said. "I
knew these guys were vicious, but this, this takes the cake.
You don't know how crazy it is working for I.A.D.,
Freeman. You don't know it when you first start, but you
soon learn that once you get in, you can't get out. I knew
this one detective who tried to go back to precinct work,
and the other cops somehow found out he was coming from
I.A.D. and when he showed up for work that first day he
found a target on his locker, with a picture of a rat with his
name on it stuck to the center of the target by a dart. He
couldn't find anybody who would work with him. Another
time someone urinated in front of his locker. He wound up
leaving the force. I mean it's tough trying to catch a
criminal cop, he knows all of our techniques, he's been
trained in them. And then, the damn division doesn't give
you the kind of support and backup you need. Frankly,
Freeman, I suspect that if we brought this tape in they
would say first of all that it was illegally obtained, and that
the talk about Dinkins was just drunken bravado. If we're
going to take Gary down, then we've got to avoid I.A.D.
roadblocks. Now, Ralph, what type of pull do you have

with the officers in the Hispanic Society, because I've got a plan and there's not much time."

Chapter Forty

"Yo', O.K., I've got to talk to you about something."

"Yeah, Okay, Freeman, wassup?"

"Man, remember those cops Larry Davis . . ."

"Adam Abdul-Hakeem."

"Oh yeah, I forgot that brotha became a muslim, my bad. As I was sayin', remember those cops that he said were sellin' drugs way back in '87. Remember? In '87 he named that cop who just testified at the Mollen Commission hearings."

"Who Dowd?"

"Nah, uh, uh Cawley. Remember, in '87 Davis named him as part of a gang of cops in the Bronx sellin' drugs and goin' around beatin' up colored folk. Well I was readin' about the hearings and it was describin' how Cawley was known by his fellow white boys in blue, as 'The Mechanic', 'cause he used his fist and feet to give people a tune-up.' (In describing his beating exploits, Cawley said that cops would use anything from their nightsticks to large flashlights to sap gloves packed with an ounce of sand - to give their beatings, an extra ounce of brutality.)

"And yo', did you know that Michael Dowd, was making so much money that he was able to buy four fuckin' houses and a $34,000 red corvette?! And these muthafuckas want us to believe that they didn't know he was corrupt! Gi-i-it the fuck outta here!" (In an ironic twist, Eric Adams served as an adviser to the otherwise colorless, or at least overwhelmingly colorless, Mollen Commission (the Commission had only one black panelist, and no Latinos). According to Adams as long Dowd operated in poor Black and Latino neighborhoods he was able to thrive, but as soon as he tried to start selling drugs in the suburbs, he got busted. As Ice Cube's menacing character raps on 'The Nigga Ya Love to Hate', as long as he was robbin' his own kind, the Blue Klux didn't mind, but when he started robbin' white folk he ended up in the pokie wit' the soap on the rope!)

"Why are you telling me this, Freeman?"

"Because I've got a cop story to tell you, and I don't want you to think that Ah'm buggin'."

Chapter Forty-one

Knowing how adventurous, and sometimes downright reckless, Freeman could be, Uncle Tom wondered if he'd done the right thing, telling him about the bust. And when he called Freeman's house, and no one answered. Tom became more concerned that Freeman was up in Washington Heights trying to scope out the bust.

Uncle Tom's instincts were right, Freeman couldn't resist, his concern for Angelita, his dislike of Gary, his distrust of cops and his journalistic instincts all combined to convince him that he at least had to see the bust. He wasn't doing any harm as far as he was concerned, after all.

Chapter Forty-two

As Freeman sat with O.K. in a corner table at Club 2000, it was hard not be distracted by the disco lights, the beautiful women and the head bobbing base. But as O.K. wondered aloud how he had ever let Freeman talk him into coming, Freeman was forced to remember why they were there. Apparently, Gary had chosen the Club as the site for the drop off because he'd figured that the dealers would be less likely to shoot him in a crowded disco, and he also knew that there wouldn't be any officers frequenting the Club to bust him if things did indeed go smoothly. As the transaction's appointed hour approached, O.K. grew ever more apprehensive about having agreed to accompany Freeman on what he deemed to be a foolhardy venture, and Freeman was getting sick of it.

"Come on, O.K., now, I tried to talk you out of comin', I shoulda never told your ass. Now you know two of us can fit in better than one, so chill, and act like you're here to have a good time."

"Okay, bet, I'll catch you later, I'm goin' to dance with that babe in the peach outfit over there."

"Come on, stop playin'."

"Ah'm just fuckin' wit' you."

"Wait a minute, what color outfit did you say?!"

"Peach. See her? Right over there."

"Oh no, turn your head."

"Why?"

Peaches and cream this wasn't. 'Murphy's Law': "whatever can go wrong will go wrong" had struck, and a second later a chill went up Freeman's back when he heard a familiar voice say: "Mira! Mira!" He tried to play it off like he didn't hear her. O.K. sensing Freeman's uneasiness, asked who she was.

"Really? Angelita's sister," he said. One could see the wheels turning, and Freeman knew what was coming next - "Yo', hook me up?" O.K.'s familiar request.

"Mira, aqui, aqui!"

"Yo' Free, we'd better go over there before she attracts attention."

"Yeah," he said with a sigh that made him sound both exhausted and defeated, "you're right."

"What you doin' here, Freeman? Angelita know?"

"Ah'm just chillin' wit' my man," Freeman said coolly, trying to look relaxed and to temper Peaches' temper.

"My name's O.K." O.K. said as he jumped in, hand extended, teeth flashing and his little man rising to stand at attention. "You wanna dance?" He asked.

"Uh, we'll be right back," Freeman said.

"Where you goin'?" Peaches asked.

"Yo', why you blowin' my rap?" An agitated O.K. whispered, as Freeman dragged him away.

"Shhhh, chill, there he go."

"Where?" O.K. asked in a quiet whisper.

"The guy over there with the shades."

As 'Peace in the valley' blasted from the speakers, adrenaline shot through Freeman's body, as he and O.K. spied Gary sitting at a table conversing with three Dominican guys.

"There it is." Freeman exclaimed as he saw one of the Dominican guys hand Gary an envelope.

Excited, Freeman moved in for a closer look and listen, earlier he'd thought that he was going to be able to jot down his observations once he got in the Club, but the security guard searching him took away his pen, seems no pens are allowed inside. He had also had to pay five dollars extra to wear his 40 Acres and A Mule baseball cap inside, well actually, ten dollars when you throw in O.K.'s five dollar cap wearing penalty as well. (O.K. was wearing a red and white Kansas City Monarchs cap. He claimed to be related to Satchel Paige.) Unfortunately for Freeman, he'd underestimated Gary, for it seems all black people don't always all look alike all the time. When Gary saw Freeman slinking by he knew something was wrong and gave Steve Violet the abort sign - that's when Steve suddenly realized that he'd seen the burly silent bodyguard sitting across from him somewhere before, it took a second for him to recall, and then he realized the 'Spic' was a cop, and with fear burning through his body he bolted toward the exit like a brotha mistakenly at a Klan meeting, with the undercover officers in hot pursuit not far behind. As Gary ran by, Freeman tripped him, he stumbled but managed to maintain his balance as he raced toward the stairs. Tom and Ralph, who had been waiting in an unmarked car parked up the block near Angelita's house listening to the transaction through a bug they'd placed at the scene before Gary's arrival, raced to the Club as soon as they heard Gary and Tom take off. As Ralph started up the steps he suddenly looked into the face of his wife's lover, Steve Violet. Ralph was overcome with rage and pounced on his tormentor who was suddenly soaked under the deluge of blows Ralph was raining on him. Then just as suddenly as it had started raining, it stopped, as the torrential downpour was interrupted by the sound of thunder, actually it was the sound of the blast of Steve Violet's gun, followed close behind by the slump, then tumble, and finally the fall of Ralph's limp body. Violet went red in the face when he saw Ralph tumble down the steps, looking back he saw that his pursuers were caught in the crowd, when he looked again to the exit, a right hand ran into his face. As he looked up from the floor, he tried to aim his gun, but a sweeping size twelve kicked it out of his hand, and another right hand plowed into his jaw. He was down for the count.

"Damn, uncle Tom, I forgot you used to box!"

"Yo', Freeman your uncle is hittin' like Tyson!"

"Thanks for the accolades fellas, but where's Gary?"

"I don't know, he was runnin' toward the steps last I saw of him, then I lost him in the crowd." Freeman explained.

"You looking for me?" They heard Gary's voice ask from somewhere above them. When they looked up, they saw Gary standing at the top of the stairs with his gun drawn, and the crowd backing away behind him. "Okay, I'm coming down now, and I'm leaving, so no fucking funny business." As Gary barked his orders he started down the steps, glancing back for a second to make sure no one was coming behind him, just long enough for Uncle Tom to make his move, but alas not long enough to succeed, and an instant later the gun fell from Uncle Tom's hand, a split second after it was stung by the lead's penetration. "I fucking told you no funny business!" Gary once again barked. "You! Come here!" Gary growled at Freeman. "Come here, C. Vernon Mason!" Gary screamed, this time pointing his gun at Freeman who grudgingly acquiesced to Gary's command. "Now, like I said, I'm getting out of here, and if I even think that anyone is even thinking about following me, Al Sharpton here has had it! Now, get the hell out of my way," he yelled at the wounded Tom and the unarmed O.K.. Gary then led Freeman down the stairs, keeping Freeman in front of him, and his gun squarely on his back, just itching to squeeze the trigger. As he walked past Tom, he spat in his face and called him a lowlife rat. Then as they reached the bottom of the stairs, he ordered Freeman to stand against the door with his hands over his head. As Gary looked down at the prone Ralph, he felt betrayed, he actually had genuine feelings for Ralph - he thought of him as a pet. Now angered at what he regarded as Ralph's betrayal, he drew back his leg to kick the downed dog; but unfortunately for Gary sometimes it's better to let sleeping dogs lie, because it is indeed true that every dog has his day - even Ralph, so as Gary's foot soared towards Ralph, Ralph's arm reached up and swept his other leg out from under him whereupon Gary flew into the air like a breakdancer who didn't know how to breakdance. Gary crashed against the floor, whereupon Freeman, O.K. and Ralph all beat the shit out of him. Literally.

"Oh shit! Ralph you're really okay." Freeman marvelled.

"Thank God for bulletproof vest. Thank God for bulletproof vest." Ralph prayed.

Chapter Forty-three

"So, Freeman, Angelita tells me you want to interview me for your paper, tell me what kind of story are you planning to write?"

"We'll, uh'm, I was planning on tying in your beating with Officer Pannel's shooting to show how even if you're a cop, if you're Black or Latino you're still not safe."

"You know Freeman the events of the last six weeks have obliterated some political cataracts that had been blurring my vision. You know, it's funny, they say the Lord works in mysterious ways, well my recent turmoil has forced me to confront issues I had chosen to ignore or denigrate. As you know, both the Hispanic Society and the

Guardians have been very supportive of me in my conflict
with the department, however, that support masks what I
see as a dangerous undercurrent of tension between Blacks
and Latinos. Like I said before, these are issues I would
not have thought of before, but Angelita's relationship with
you, and my experiences in this whole ordeal have forced
me to look at these issues. Although both the Hispanic
Society and the Guardians are supporting me, I see that
when it comes to citywide politics, there is a deep division
that I fear may turn the city over to the hands of that man,
Giuliani. Now, hear me Freeman, I was at the police
demonstration against the Civilian Complaint Review
Board, hmmph, to think I was once proud of that, but
anyway, I know those police, I know how racist they are,
I allowed myself to be blind before but knowing what I
know, I cannot be silent. The reason I am saying all of this
is because in my interactions with the Hispanic Society I
discovered that there was a tremendous internal fight as to
whether they would support Giuliani or Dinkins. It was a
struggle but finally, in June they voted 42 to 40 to back
Dinkins."

    "Damn, that was close!" Freeman exclaimed,
somewhat shocked that it would be that close. He'd just
assumed that they would be supporting Dinkins, no
question. "Who's the PBA backin'?", Freeman asked
already sure he knew what the answer would be.

    "Don't make me laugh. You know those white
officers are pumped for Giuliani. Most of them don't even
live in the city. Don't be so surprised, though, Freeman,
many of the older officers remember Ben Ward as being
hostile to Latinos, and I believe that some of the hostility
toward Ward is carrying over against Dinkins. Now, if you
want, you can do another article on police brutality, but I
think you can do something much more constructive."

"What's that?"

"Well, as I see it Blacks and Latinos comprise a majority of the city's population. What are we going to do to form coalitions to gain real power in this city? So that we can see to it that the police are policed for real. What are we gonna do? I say your next issue should be entitled 'Dinkins, Blacks, Latinos and the future of New York City Politics'! Moreover, I think your paper should sponsor a forum around the mayoral election, and politics in the City in general."

Freeman was stunned, he could not believe that this was the same guy who only two months before, wouldn't have even dared go near a Hispanic Society meeting, who would never have used the term Latino, after all he was 'Spanish', who would never have acknowledged that Latinos had any African heritage, and now here he was schooling *him!*

"Ralph . . . "

"Rafael."

"Rafael, I have to say, first, I can't believe this is the same guy I met two months ago."

"Shit happens, things change."

"Well, you've given me a lot to think about, and what you've said does make a lot of sense. I just don't know about this forum shit though, you know how hard it is to get colored folk together."

"Well, if we don't get together, be prepared to hear 'Mayor Giuliani' for the next four years."

"Damn, that's not a pleasant thought."

"It may not be a pleasant thought, but it's reality. Well, anyway, you think about it. I've got to go. I've got a date." He said with a self-satisfied smile.

"A date?!" Exclaimed a shocked Freeman.

"Yes, a date. Remember, man does not live by plátanos alone." As Rafael walked out the door, Freeman's curiosity was piqued, and he anxiously waited for the door to close, so that he could get the scoop from Angelita - who could see the interest burning in Freeman's eyes.

"Okay Angelita, fess up, whose your brother goin' out wit'?"

"I don't know." She said, rather unconvincingly, a fact Freeman did not miss.

"Aw c'mon mi hermosa mujer. Quien es tu hermano going out wit'?"

"You wouldn't believe me."

"Try me."

"I'm tellin' you, you wouldn't believe me."

"Just try me."

"Okay."

"Who?"

"Who? Toni Braxton."

"Yeah, right, now who, come on."

"He's goin' out wit' this Haitian woman."

"Get outta here. Your moms must be havin' a fit."

"You could say that."

"Boy, that's funny, I just remember the first time I saw him, and he was fawnin' over, uh'm, what's her name?"

"Olga."

"Oh yeah Olga. Whatever happened to her?"

"I don't know, he never talks about it an as far as I know she's never called." Angelita had no way of knowing that Olga was too busy dealing with problems of her own to have thought about calling the de Cimarrones. First off, she had the little problem of noncitizenship and she was trying her best to stay one step ahead of the I.N.S. demons she kept in her head by melting into the Russian immigrant community of Brighton Beach in Brooklyn. Meanwhile, she also had to contend with her growing suspicion that she was pregnant combined with her ignorance as to the identity of the baby's father, coupled with her confusion as to whom to hope was indeed the daddy. She had learned, even in her short stay in America that a white baby would have substantial competitive advantages over a "little brown bomber." "What am I going to do?" She asked herself again and again. She considered an abortion, just in case her little bundle of joy turned out to be a bit overdone, but she was afraid that it would tip off her immigrant status. She clung to the hope that the child was Steve Violet's (it was) - surely this would prove her love for him, and cement their relationship, she believed or rather hoped, even though since she had been tossed by Raphael, Steve had yet to return one of her phone calls.

"So, what did my brother say about the story?" Angelita asked.

"He gave me a lot to think about. About the future of the City, about the future of Black and Latino people in the City, and how we're going to move forward or get left behind."

Chapter Forty-four

Freeman barely had time to celebrate Gary's downfall before he was brutally and painfully reminded that there was a much bigger, stronger and intractable enemy to confront - the debilitating effects of the belief that whites have a monopoly on all opportunity. It was this belief that continually beat Freeman and his cohorts down as they sought to get out the vote on election day, only to be continuously rebuffed by Black and Latino voters who didn't think that their vote mattered anyway.

The night of the election, Freeman was at Dinkins' election eve party. As the late night polls foretold Guiliani's impending victory, Freeman felt the electricity and excitement that had filled the room moments before, when Mayor Dinkins had momentarily taken the lead, evaporate, as the latest polls confirmed Dinkins' defeat. Anger swelled inside of him. He felt his breaths get stronger and longer as he watched his father, with controlled anger and professorial sophistication, explain to a reporter what role he thought, race had played in the outcome.

A short time later, Freeman's father was disgusted, amused and a little bit jealous as he watched Guiliani's acceptance speech and was greeted by the sight of Tom. There he was in all his glory on the podium behind Guiliani, beaming like that Black guy on the rice box, as the Mayor-elect spoke of his vision for the future.

Freeman's father had to laugh. He remembered that even when they were little kids, his brother was always a great schemer.

The next day as Freeman read the accounts of Guiliani's victory, he became enraged at the articles and editorials suggesting that if racism did play a role in the election, it was Black racism manifested by the large Black vote Dinkins received. He felt compelled to respond, and vented his anger on the pages of The Shield, in an editorial exposing some of the biased coverage regarding the racially charged campaign. In a nod to Biko, he signed off using his hero's pseudonym.

Epilogue

> It was the worse possible outcome -
> Rudy Giuliani winning narrowly,
> with virtually no increase in his
> black or Hispanic support since
> 1989. A mayor who owes his margin of
> victory to conservative middle-class
> whites who voted simultaneously to
> leave the city through Staten
> Island's secession has no clear
> mandate to govern.
>
> Jim Sleeper, Daily News
> November 3, 1993

FEAR OF A BLACK PLANET

This one goes out to Bill Reel, William F. Buckley, and most of all Eric Breindel of the, the paper Chuck D. said wasn't worth the paper it was printed on.

Recently there has been a spate of articles ridiculing any suggestion that race played a role in the recent defeat of David N. Dinkins, New York City's first Black mayor; and arguing essentially, that if racism were at play, it was the Black vote for Dinkins, not the white vote for Giuliani.

In line with these specious arguments Eric Breindel recently published an article in the Post attacking Lani Guinier for suggesting that racism played a role in Dinkins' failure to secure reelection in a city where Democrats outnumber Republicans 5 to 1. Breindel argues that Guinier ignores the fact that Dinkins is an incumbent and that incumbents tend to be judged on their record. He also charges that Prof. Guinier ignored the fact that Dinkins got a "significant" number of white votes in 1989. In his defense, I must admit that Mr. Breindel does admit that white racism would cost Dinkins some votes: "How much is "some"?"   You ask. I don't know, let's ask Mr. Breindel.

I would also like to ask Mr. Breindel to explain why, if Dinkins' low appeal to white voters can be explained by a judgment of his performance, why then Mr. Breindel did Dinkins as the Democratic candidate, in a city where among white voters Democrats vastly outnumber Republicans, did Dinkins, without a record as an incumbent, win only 27% of the white vote in 1989? Why was Giuliani, a Republican with no governing experience, showered with 70% of the white vote in their first meeting? Please explain that Mr. Breindel.

Breindel doesn't stop there, however, no, he has to attack Prof. Guinier's other "misrepresentation" to use his "generous" term. Guinier's other "misrepresentation" Breindel asserts was her statement that Latinos and Blacks often vote for whites. Breindel writes that while this claim has some merit with regard to Latinos, the same cannot be said of Blacks (shame on them). And then to prove his claim, he points to polls showing Dinkins with over 90% of the Black vote. It seems Mr. Breindel is angry that some raise the issue of white racism, while no suggestion of Black racism is raised to explain Black support for Dinkins.

Perhaps Mr. Breindel is ignorant of recent New York City mayoral electoral history. Perhaps Mr. Breindel is ignorant of the fact that the overwhelming majority of Blacks registered in the City are registered as Democrats. Perhaps Mr. Breindel is ignorant of the fact that the overwhelming mass of whites registered in the City are registered as Democrats. Perhaps Mr. Breindel is ignorant of that fact that this is a Democratic city. Perhaps he's just plain ignorant.

The fallacies of Breindel's contentions are manifest in several particulars. First off, as noted above, the overwhelming plurality of Black New Yorkers are Democrats, and pull the Democratic lever unless a compelling reason to do otherwise presents itself (D'Amato v. Abrams?). Secondly, just two short mayoral elections ago Black New Yorkers did indeed vote for a white candidate, Ed Koch, when presented with a Black alternative, Denny Farrell. In the 1985 Democratic primary then-Mayor Koch won 56 of the 60 Assembly Districts in the City, while his opponents, Carol Bellamy won one, and Mr. Farrell won three - the 70th and 71st in Harlem and Washington Heights - his home base, and the 29th in Queens. On the other hand, in absolute contradistinction to Breindel's malicious misrepresentation Koch won most predominantly Black districts by margins of up to 2 to 1 and Latino districts by up to 3 to 1. In the thirteen assembly districts with the highest percentage of Black voters, Koch garnered almost 42% of the vote, a figure Dinkins never approached in the white community. And in the 1985 general election, I'll have you know Mr. Breindel, that the former Mayor won eighty-eight percent of the Black vote.

In the final analysis, Dinkins - the lifelong Democrat, the quintessential clubhouse player, up-through-the-ranks politician was betrayed by white Democrats such as Robert Wagner, Jr. and Ed Koch, both of whom backed Giuliani.

Don't be fooled by those who decry Black bloc voting while ignoring the essential racial, ethnic and gender political calculus of Giuliani's (con)fusion campaign. Giuliani's strategy of running with Badillo and Alter was nothing but the convergence, with a slight twist, of previously hostile Badillo and Koch strategies. In 1988 a politically vulnerable Mayor Koch talked about campaigning with black or Hispanic running mates, as a sign of his recognition of the changing face of the City's electorate. A New York Times' article quoted Koch as saying that most Hispanics in New York are Puerto Rican, so his Latino running mate would probably be Puerto Rican. This from a man who virulently derided the idea of quotas!? Talk about putting figure heads above substantive power and making a purely ethnically based appeal. The proposal represented Koch's futile attempt to launch a preemptive strike against Dinkins' mayoral bid. As a matter of fact, Koch recommended specifically that a minority run, not for his office, but for Comptroller (at the time Koch was at odds with then Comptroller Harrison Goldin). So what does the original thinking Giuliani do in 1993? Bingo! You've got it - Badillo for Comptroller. Of course this was in line with sentiment expressed by Badillo in 1981 as to how to best defeat Koch. Badillo was intrigued by Cuomo's strong showing as the Liberal party candidate against Koch in 1977, and began to kick around the idea of having an Italian run for mayor. Badillo said that New Yorkers vote ethnically, anyway, and that Koch had already lost the Black and Puerto Rican vote. "Add the Italians and he's through."

So in 1993 the calculations of Badillo and Koch converged on behalf of Giuliani. An Italian mayoral candidate, a Puerto Rican candidate for Comptroller, and a Jewish person, who also happened to be a woman, for Public Advocate.

To paraphrase Badillo of 1981, Dinkins had already lost the Italian and Jewish vote, 'add the Puerto Ricans and he's through.' In exit polling in 1989 Dinkins won 67% of the Latino vote, in 1993 60%. The ties that bind held, but the rope was frayed in the process.

Frank Talk

ORDER FORM

Credit Card orders: call (800) 247-6553. Please have your card ready.

Fax Orders: (419) 281-6883.

Postal Orders: Send check or money order to I Write What I Like, Inc., P.O. Box 30, New York, NY 10268-0030. USA. Checks are payable to I Write What I Like, Inc. (718) 398-0595.

Sales tax:
      Please add 8.25% for books shipped to New York State addresses.

Shipping:
Book Rate $2.50 for the first book 75 cents for each additional book.
(Surface shipping may take three to four weeks)
Air Mail: $3.50 per book.

Please send me ____ copy(ies) of 'Do Plátanos Go Wit' Collard Greens?'.

Name: _____

Address: _____

      _____

      _____

      _____